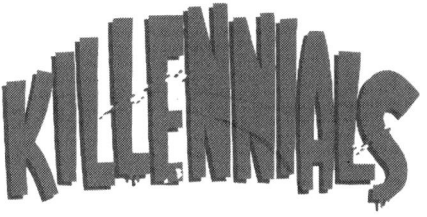

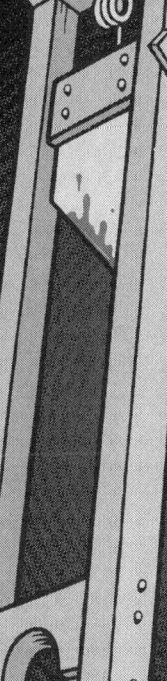

KILLENNIALS

MARTY BECKERMAN

This is a work of fiction. Characters, places, and incidents are either products of the author's imagination or are used fictitiously.

Copyright © 2018 by Marty Beckerman. All rights reserved. This book may not be reproduced or transmitted in any form or by any means without permission from the publisher, except in the case of brief passages embodied in reviews and critical articles.

Cover design by Danny Hellman

ISBN-10: 0-9700629-8-2

ISBN-13: 978-0-9700629-8-7

For N.V.

"The duty of youth is to challenge corruption."
—Kurt Cobain

"[M]ost revolutions have two goals. One is to destroy an old form of society and the other is to set up the new form of society envisioned by the revolutionaries. … As for the negative consequences of eliminating industrial society—well, you can't eat your cake and have it too. To gain one thing you have to sacrifice another."
—Theodore Kaczynski

1969

"Politicians say that North Vietnam is evil, but *real* evil is sending us off to die at eighteen and not letting us vote until we're twenty-one."

Mitchell Oldman stood on the Main Hall steps of Logan Frost University, a bullhorn in one hand, his shoulder-length hair swaying in the breeze. All of the students on the quad below wore tie-dye, beads, and other counterculture accoutrements. They looked up to him as if he were a wise man possessed of some ancient, prophetic knowledge. Like Dylan's fans. Like Lennon's fans. *Like Manson's family*, he tried not to think.

"Because if the youth had a say," Mitchell continued, "it'd all come crashing down—the draft, the oppression, the *system*."

His fellow protesters applauded. All of them had lost friends and family in Southeast Asia, and for what? Tricky Dick's ego trip?

"We'll stay right here, hand-in-hand, as long as necessary..." Mitchell took a seat on the steps and gestured for everybody to link arms. "Who has the power?"

"*We have the power!*"

"Youth power!"

"*Youth pow—*"

The stomping of jackboots diverted their attention. Police had arrived, holding riot shields and nightsticks. The Man's foot soldiers, ready to enforce obedience.

"Disperse now," said the commanding officer. "This is your only warning."

"Or stay..." Another cop grinned. "I'd like an excuse to bash in some longhair skulls."

The students, encircled and frightened, all looked to Mitchell for direction; some people were born leaders. "Never submit to these fascist pigs," he told them. "Never trust *anyone* over thirty."

A concussive blow to the face as police moved in. Mitchell fell to the ground. Bloodied. Silenced.

CHAPTER ONE

1.

Olivia walked up the Main Hall steps, texting a friend on her iPhone and listening to Spotify's Discover Weekly playlist.

Prepped all night for my tenure-track hearing...its go time, she typed and sent. *It's, stupid autocorrect. Anyway, I've been an adjunct prof here for a DECADE. My student reviews are ★★★★★ out of ★★★★★. And Dad would never vote against me.*

Olivia saw an older colleague drop a plastic Starbucks cup, with a plastic straw, into the trashcan. She took the cup out and then placed it in a recycling bin directly adjacent.

"Even tiny actions can fight global warming," Olivia said.

The baby boomer laughed. "Oh, I *like* the milder winters."

Olivia shook her head, dismayed. She did want coffee now, though—to counteract the zero sleep—and approached the espresso stand in the lobby.

"Give me a skinny caramel frappe, fair-trade sustainable blend, no straw," she said to the student barista. "And I'll have the avocado toast."

"That's four dollars for the coffee..." The barista entered Olivia's order into a tablet. "And sixteen dollars for the toast."

"Six*teen*?" Olivia said. "For a slice of bread and half a Hass? Ugh...okay, it's a special day."

She swiped her credit card. Declined.

"Do you have cash?" the barista said. "We also take Bitcoin."

"My physical *and* digital wallets are empty," Olivia said, slumping from mortification. She appreciated life's small pleasures, but couldn't afford many of them.

"You need to pay somehow..."

Olivia took a breath. "How much is *regular* toast?"

"A dollar," the barista said.

"And how much is an avocado?"

"Also a dollar."

"Fine..." Olivia scrounged together quarters, dimes, nickels, and pennies from the bottom of her bag. "I'll spread it myself."

2.

Vintage propaganda posters decorated the classroom walls—euphoric farmers holding bountiful harvests, determined proletarians building the future with cubist sledgehammers—but all of the students gazed at the bladeless guillotine that Olivia had snagged at a Craigslist weirdo's yard sale.

"All right, class, welcome to History, Society, and Revolution..." Olivia placed breakfast on her desk for later. "I'm your professor, Olivia. *Adjunct* professor, I mean, but alllllllmost tenure-track, knock on wood." She tapped the guillotine with her knuckles. "We have a lot of material to cover this semester, from—"

A student raised his hand. "Don't we call professors by their *last* name?" he said.

"Formal is hardly my jam," Olivia said. "Think of me like a cool, slightly-but-not-*that*-much older sister. Now, over this semester we'll compare and contrast revolutions in France, Russia, Iran, and Ch—"

Another student uploaded live video from her phone while applying cosmetics. "And be sure to use the *original* Beauty Blender—not a knockoff—on sale right now if you follow the link in the description," she said. "Don't forget to blend your neck so there's no harsh line."

The other students whispered: "*Whoa, is that Makeup Meg?*" "*OMG, she's* super *famous.*" "*Let's all get selfies with her.*"

"Hey," Olivia said to Meg, "we all love dicking around on social media, but let's put the phone away during class, okay?"

"But I'm livestreaming to my eighteen million followers *right now*."

Olivia took Meg's phone and placed it beside the avocado.

"Thanks for watching, everybody," Meg yelled so her voice would carry to the viewers. "Click to subscribe and be sure to follow me on Snapchat, Twitter, and Insta!" She twitched without her phone, feeling around for it out of habit, as if she had a ghost limb.

Olivia rolled her eyes. "Now, as I was saying, the material we'll cover this semester—" Oinking from the back of the room. "Is that a goddamn *pig*?"

"It's my emotional support pig," a student said. "I'll *literally* die if we're separated."

"Not a correct use of 'literally,' but sure, okay,

whatever." Olivia sighed. "Everybody just take a syllabus." She distributed a stack of papers.

"Professor, I'm calling you out!" said yet another student. "That's a waste of paper. You could send the file to us digitally and save trees. Do you hate trees?"

Olivia had gone from eco-shamer to eco-shamed. "That's a great point," she said. "What's your name?"

"Nikki."

"That's a *great* point, Nikki, and exactly what this course is about: changing the status quo by raising your voice. Progress isn't made by the march of time alone, but rather by people who speak up, refuse to back down, and *keep* doing it, because yesterday's radicals can become tomorrow's establishment."

Olivia lifted the avocado from her desk.

"Let's go around the room," she said. "When you get the avocado, introduce yourself and tell us your favorite revolutionary."

Olivia tossed the avocado—with perfect aim—to Nikki.

"Wow, good throw," Nikki said.

"Varsity softball," Olivia said. "Still got it."

"So, like I said, I'm Nikki, and my favorite revolutionary is…hmm…does Susan B. Anthony count?"

"You better *B.*-lieve it."

The students groaned at Olivia's pun, albeit with growing affection. Nikki passed the avocado in the direction of identical twin brothers, both hulking, tattooed jocks with their hair styled in man buns.

"Yo, I'm Jackson," said one. "This is my bro, Ash."

"And your favorite revolutionary?" Olivia asked.

"Uh...like the Revolutionary War?" Jackson said. "So, George Washington, I guess? 'Murica."

"I'm calling you out!" Nikki said. "He's not much of a revolutionary if he *owned human beings*."

"Sorry, that's wack...uh...Alexander Hamilton?" Jackson said. "I saw the musical."

"That's acceptable," Nikki said. "Lin-Manuel is dope."

Jackson handed the avocado to Ash.

"Like my bro said, I'm Ash, and I love me some Beerrrrrrrnnnnnnnnnnie Sannnnnnnnnderrrrrrrrrs."

"Still feelin' the *Bern*, yo," Jackson added.

"It's cool if they're from today, right?" Ash said. "Not hundreds of years ago?"

"Of course," Olivia said. "Great choice."

"You hear that, bro?" Ash said to Jackson. "'Great choice.'"

"That's fire, bro," Jackson said.

"'Fire'...?" Olivia said.

"Not fire like *bad*," Ash explained. "Fire like dope."

Olivia nodded. So this was obsolescence.

Ash tossed the avocado to Meg.

"Heyyyy, you probably know me already—I'm Makeup Meg, and I'd say my favorite revolutionary is either PewDiePie or Jenna Marbles, because they *revolutionized* the YouTube game."

"Er...'A' for effort," Olivia said, returning Meg's phone.

"Thank. You." Meg passed the avocado to the next student.

"Hi, my name is Pablo," he said, nervous and meek. "I really like Mahatma Gandhi and Martin Luther King, Jr., because they both showed how nonviolence is the best way to change people's minds."

"That's so inspiring," Olivia said.

"That's so *wrong*," said the student beside Pablo, grabbing the avocado. He was intense, too intense, looking rail-thin yet scrappy like a rabid stray. "I'm Caleb, and the greatest revolutionary of our time is Theodore Kaczynski, because he showed the exact opposite."

"*Ted* Kaczynski?" Olivia said. "The *Unabomber*...?"

"Have you read his manifesto?" Caleb said. "It's brilliant. He wasn't just some kook in a cabin. He predicted *all* of society's problems: climate change, internet addiction, robots taking workers' jobs...he tried to *warn* us. No wonder the FBI threw him in jail."

"Yeah," Olivia said, "because he was a terrorist?"

She knew this guy was going to be trouble. What is it about a certain kind of eighteen-year-old boy too smart and angry for his own good—or anybody else's?

"'Terrorist' is just another way of saying 'freedom fighter,'" Caleb said. "Or as Mr. Kaczynski put it, 'In order to get our message before the public with some chance of making a lasting impression, we've had to kill people.'"

"Okay. Wow." Olivia blinked. "Jesus Christ, kid."

"*Caleb*...I haven't been a 'kid' since puberty."

Olivia took the avocado back. "Let's move on, shall we, Caleb?"

"*You're* the one with a guillotine in your classroom," Caleb said.

"No blade. For educational purposes only. And speaking of education..." Olivia set the avocado on her desk again and opened a history textbook. "Let's dive in and flip to Chapter One."

None of the students had the textbook except for Pablo, who looked around the room, embarrassed.

"Um, guys...?" Olivia said. "What's up?"

"I'm calling you out!" Nikki said. "'Guys' is a patriarchal and male-normative way to address people who don't all identify as such."

"Right. We want everybody to feel welcome here. So, what's up, people?"

"Professor Olivia," Ash said, "that textbook costs *four hundred bucks*. My bro and I already work nights and weekends to pay off tuition, yo. We're going into debt for the rest of our lives just to get entry-level jobs."

The other students murmured in agreement.

"Sixty thousand dollars each year plus dorm and meal plan?" Jackson said. "It's extortion! Makes me wanna *crush* something."

"I hear it," Olivia said.

"Obviously you hear it," Caleb sneered, "because you're *profiting* from it. You and your rich, happy family...I googled you, dean's daughter."

"Whoa, Caleb," Olivia said. "First off, *I* still have seventy thou in grad school debt myself. And did you hear when I said I'm an *adjunct*? That means the university doesn't even technically employ me; I'm an 'independent contractor.' No health benefits, no overtime, no paid vacation...I'm getting just as screwed as you are, okay?" She paused. "As for my family, 'happy' is an overstatement."

"At least you *have* a family," Caleb said. "Not everyone is so privileged. Besides, aren't you 'alllllllmost tenure-track'? Soon to be another cog in the revenue-generating machine?"

"Soon to be an equal," Olivia said. "Soon to be *respected*. Kid."

"'Yesterday's radicals *can* become tomorrow's establishment.'"

3.

Olivia strutted into the staff lounge for her academic interview, brimming with confidence and carrying a binder filled with notes. Her big day had finally arrived. The other faculty members, nearly all in their sixties and seventies—wrinkled, paunchy, and gray—sat around a long conference table. Olivia couldn't remember most of their names, instead dubbing them Professor Old White Guy #1, #2, and #3.

Just a formality, right? Olivia told herself. *This is basically a done deal.*

She took a seat next to her favorite boomer colleague, Linda—presently wearing a rainbow headband and a "MAKE LOVE, NOT WAR" T-shirt—who chaired the Department of Art and Design and had never lost her old-school hippie free spirit.

"I shouldn't tell you how I'm voting before your presentation," Linda whispered to Olivia, "but you're overdue. I received tenure when I was even younger than you are now. It's just how things were done back then."

"Thanks, Linda," Olivia said. "You're hashtag #Amazeballs."

"Pardon me…?"

"You're the best."

Olivia recalled Ash and Jackson's slang from earlier in the day: *Not fire like bad…fire like dope.* Maybe all generations were doomed to misunderstand one another.

Her father, Dean Oldman, entered the room. The other professors stood as a sign of respect.

"We scheduled this hearing to consider the rank of assistant professor for our adjunct colleague Olivia Oldman," said the dean, taking his place at the head of the table. "Now, I can't pretend to be neutral in this matter…" Polite laughter all around. "Objectively, however, Olivia has made an undeniable impact on hundreds of students over the past…has it been ten years now?"

"Sure has, Pops," Olivia said.

Ten years of grading essays until midnight. Ten years of publishing research in the most prestigious journals. Ten years of proving herself worthy.

"Goodness, time flies," Dean Oldman said. "I'm so proud to call Olivia my daughter."

The professors all smiled. Olivia shifted in her chair, counting the seconds.

"But in that time," Dean Oldman said, voice growing somber, "we've extended tenure-track positions to no other adjunct staff. Our finance committee crunched the numbers again this morning; we *still* lack the resources. I must regretfully cancel this open position. My apologies for not informing all of you sooner. Olivia, if you still want to give your presentation, just for fun...I know you worked hard on it."

Olivia's face dropped. She had worked for *months* on it, had prepared hours of material. "What? I...but...*hold up.*" She felt a numb stupefaction. "The job I'm interviewing for doesn't *exist* anymore?"

"Perhaps next year," Dean Oldman said, "if the budget allows." His expression implied that it would not allow.

"About time these spoiled millennials heard the word 'no,'" muttered P.O.W.G. #3, the one who liked milder winters. His derisive comment received chuckles from around the room, minus Olivia and Linda.

"Uh oh," said P.O.W.G. #2 with a belly laugh, "that sounded like a microaggression to *my* sensitive ears."

"Even worse than wearing a Bob Marley wig or Indian headdress for Halloween," said P.O.W.G. #1. "Cultural appropriation...the horror! The horror!"

"Baby better call the waaaaaaambulance," said P.O.W.G. #3. Even Dean Oldman cracked a smile, breaking his precious decorum.

It's all such a joke to them, Olivia thought. *My life, others' feelings, the dying ecosystem...what* isn't *a joke to them?*

"Well, I object...this is absurd and unfair," Linda said, patting Olivia's hand on the table. "Our generation of scholars received tenure—the *opportunity* for it—as a matter of course, but we're making the next generation wait until we die off to start their lives? How can you all sit here and say, 'We've got ours, screw you'? To the *future*?"

"That's enough, Linda," Dean Oldman said. "We're not saying 'screw you,' just 'not yet.' They can wait a little longer. Patience is a virtue."

Olivia's blood boiled. Why would her father humiliate her like this? She had worked so hard, sacrificed so much, by any standard.

"'Patience'?" Olivia found her voice. "You want to lecture me about *patience* when I've waited a fucking *decade*?" She stood, repressing tears. "When I'm barely making minimum wage and you geezers are enjoying your McMansions?"

"My home isn't a 'mansion,'" said P.O.W.G. #2.

"It's better than still living at your dad's house!"

Olivia stormed out of the staff lounge and slammed the door behind her, but then reopened it.

"You're dope, though, Linda."

She slammed the door again.

CHAPTER TWO

4.

As dusk fell, Olivia sobbed on a bench outside of the Main Hall. She hadn't seen her father's betrayal coming. The careerist knife that he'd stuck in her back hurt more, not less, with each passing hour.

"Professor Olivia?" Pablo said, walking by her. "You look so sad."

Olivia wiped away her tears. "Hey...Pablo, right? You're the one who had the textbook."

"Only because of my scholarship—but I didn't want to make it awkward for everyone in class. They all seemed so angry about it."

Olivia sniffled. "They weren't angry at you,

bud," she said. "Just at...well, me, and the school, and all of the *bullshit* screwing up our lives."

She burst out crying again.

"What's wrong, Professor?"

"It's...boring adult stuff."

"But you're still young!"

"Not like you," Olivia said. "Not young enough to be a dreamer anymore."

"That's funny...I *am* a DREAMer," Pablo said. "My parents brought me across the border when I was a baby."

"Oh, I didn't mean it like—" Olivia paused. "You should be hanging with your friends, Pablo, not consoling your sad-sack teacher. Go party."

"There's a party tonight, I heard...I haven't made any friends yet, though."

"Crash it. Make friends. People will love you, Pablo. You're such a sweet kid...*man.*"

"You can call me a 'kid,' Professor Olivia. I don't care about it like, um, some people."

They shared a smile.

5.

Olivia parked her 2006 Toyota Prius—199,000 miles, musty smell, useless Bluetooth that recognized phone calls but not music—in the driveway next to her father's current-year sport utility vehicle.

Keep polluting the Earth with that gas-guzzler, Pops, she thought. *You won't be around long enough to see the oceans drown civilization, so what do you care about your carbon emissions?*

Olivia slammed her fists against the steering wheel. "Asshole. Asshole. *Asshole.*"

She stepped out of the hybrid. An envelope in the mailbox, addressed to her from a collections agency, had a "FINAL NOTICE" stamp.

Albert Einstein was right, Olivia thought. *Compound interest is a motherfucker.*

She opened the front door of the house. Dean Oldman read a newspaper in the living room; it had been printed the night prior, an eternity ago by modern media standards. A front-page story carried the headline, "Banking Subcommittee Chairwoman Ellis: Debt Forgiveness 'Won't Happen On My Watch.'"

"Stock market is way up," Dean Oldman said. "This economy is red hot. Thank God I bought that Exxon stock when I did."

"Wow, Dad," Olivia said, "I'm so excited for all of the equities that I don't own in the retirement account that I don't have *because you pay me like an indentured servant.* And seriously, who still gets their news from the paper?"

"Honey, let's talk about earlier..."

"I've heard you talk enough for the rest of my natural life."

"How would it look? We're in a hiring freeze, but oh, the dean's daughter gets a special pass? My own flesh and blood is granted tenure-track when I've had to deny it to so many others? We'd be chased off campus with torches. Nepotism! Privilege!"

Olivia flung the collections envelope at him. "A living wage isn't a 'privilege,' Dad, it's a human right."

"Last time I checked, you're 'living' just fine under my roof," Dean Oldman said. "A less charitable father might kick you out to fend for yourself."

"Do you think I *want* to be sleeping in my childhood bedroom deep into my thirties?"

"*I* bought a starter home right out of college." The dean harrumphed. "Pulled myself up by my bootstraps."

"I *wish* I could do that," Olivia said. "Know what a 'starter home' is gonna be for my generation? *Our graves*, because it's the only land we'll ever have."

"You could've married that billionaire you dated in college..." Dean Oldman flipped the paper to a business section feature about the dating app

SwypeRite. He pointed at an Associated Press photo of its CEO, Travis Zachmann. "This one, yes?"

Olivia felt her stomach churn. "Travis wasn't a billionaire *then*. You don't think I regret breaking up with him?" She caught herself and amped up the indignation. "But really, suggesting that I marry a man for his money is some 1950s shit, Dad."

"What's wrong with that? America was a great country then."

"Except for the segregation and McCarthyism and women not being able to work and gay people being thrown in prison, you mean?"

"It wasn't all bad..." The dean let out an exasperated sigh; they'd had this discussion countless times. "I'm sorry that life isn't what you'd hoped, Olivia, but you were so set on a worthless major. This is what happens when every kid gets a participation trophy."

"*You* gave me those trophies, 'Coach,'" Olivia said. "At the end of every softball season. My entire childhood, you told me to follow my dreams."

"Well, dreams don't always come true, do they?" Dean Oldman's voice filled with bitterness. "When that happens, we need a Plan B. And the B doesn't stand for 'bitching.'"

"Ugh, hearing your lectures now is somehow even worse than when I was a teenager."

"We're academics..." Dean Oldman shrugged. "Lecturing is what we do."

Olivia took a framed, yellowed newspaper clipping off the wall. A black-and-white photo showed Dean Oldman as a young man, leading the sit-in on the steps of the Main Hall.

"Whatever happened to *this* guy?" Olivia said. "The one who stood up for what's right even if it meant getting beaten to a pulp? The one Mom married? Would *he* treat *his* workers like garbage? When did you become such an old, fat sellout?"

Dean Oldman snatched the clipping from Olivia and placed it back on the wall. "Don't bring your mother into this," he said. "That's petty, even for you."

I wish she'd lived and you'd *gotten cancer,* Olivia thought, immediately hating herself for it.

"I may be older and fatter, Olivia," Dean Oldman continued, "but I didn't sell out...I grew up. You should try it sometime. Have you ever considered that, as people mature, they learn from experience? Gain wisdom? That maybe your elders have a little more perspective than you do?"

"My 'elders' are complacent, greedy, wasteful, jingoistic, and bigoted," Olivia said.

An EDM beat grew audible from outside. Dean

Oldman opened the window curtain. "Am I hearing...music?"

6.

In the backyard Pablo weaved between dozens of students who drank from blue plastic cups and vaped sativa-dominant strains. Everybody had found their friend groups already, it seemed. He felt agonizingly out of place. Why was human interaction so difficult? The only friend that he'd made at college so far was Professor Olivia.

"Oops...sorry!" Pablo had bumped into a mountain of muscle, spilling its beer.

"Watch where you're going," Jackson said. "You want us to *crush* you?" He took a threatening half-step towards Pablo, but Ash held him back.

"Bro, *chill*," Ash said. "Accident."

"Hey, you guys are in my history class," Pablo said. "With Professor Olivia? She's so cool, isn't she?"

"Oh yeah, she's fuckin' hot as hell," Jackson said. "Like, for an older chick."

"That's objectification, bro," Ash said. "We should be trying to move past that kind of talk as a gender and shit. Didn't you listen to those podcasts I sent?"

"So, uh, you're brothers?" Pablo said. "I don't have any siblings, but I've always wanted one. It must be great."

"Yeah, it's all right," Jackson said.

"Just 'all right'?" Ash said. "That's all I get?"

"Nah, bro, I'm just messin' with you," Jackson said. "You're my *boy*, bro."

"You're *my* boy."

They bumped chests and then chugged their beers. Ash gave his not-quite-empty cup to Pablo.

"Yo, little bro," Ash said, "have the rest of my beer."

Pablo held the cup but didn't sip from it. "Oh, thanks, but my scholarship...I can't risk it. I'm not judging you guys, though." He saw Meg and Nikki nearby. "Hey, aren't they in our class, too?"

Meg uploaded another livestream from her phone.

"Heyyyyyy, Meg Nation," she said. "We're coming to you *live* from the most lit party in Logan Frost history, and you've got a front-row seat."

Nikki tapped Meg on the shoulder. Meg tried to ignore the interruption, but—as it continued—hit pause on her screen.

"What do you *want*?" Meg said. "Why can't I livestream in peace today?"

"We're all drinking underage and you're *recording* us?" Nikki said. "You're supposed to hide that shit, not share it to the entire internet."

"My fans would never snitch on me," Meg said. "All they have is love for me."

Pablo, walking towards them, wanted to defuse the tension, always his natural instinct even though his mother had warned him about the hazards of trying to break up fights; if you were undocumented in this country—especially now—you kept your head down. "Hi, classmates," he said. "How do you like the party? Are you having a fun party time?"

"It's...fine?" Nikki said.

Jackson turned to Ash and laughed. "This little bro needs to work on his icebreaker, yo."

A pyrotechnic crackle in the sky. They looked up. Students on the roof were lighting fireworks.

"Um," Meg said to Nikki, "I don't think we can 'hide that shit,' anyway."

7.

"That's it..." Dean Oldman lifted the receiver of his landline phone. "I'm calling the police."

"Come *on*, Dad, give the kids a break," Olivia said. "*You* never partied in college?"

"That was different."

"How?"

"We were expanding our minds, challenging conformity, tuning in," Dean Oldman said. "It was a political act, a *spiritual* act. Across the street? That's hedonism."

"Yeah," Olivia sneered, "I'm sure rolling around in the mud, tripping balls, and having sex with any nearby hole was *super* spiritual."

Dean Oldman dialed 911. The operator answered, "What's your emergency?"

"I'd like to report an out-of-control party across the street," Dean Oldman said. "They certainly don't appear to be twenty-one. Need the address?"

"We can trace it, sir. Officers will arrive soon."

"Thank you. Law and order, that's what I like to hear."

The dean set the receiver back down.

"Ugh, you're pathetic," Olivia said.

"Ever heard of a legal concept called *in loco parentis*?" Dean Oldman said. "University employees are responsible for students' safety. If we fail in that duty—for example, if they drink themselves to death in full view of our house—then their families can sue for negligence. Your student loans would be a drop in *that* ocean of debt."

Olivia opened the front door. "Oh wait, I'm *not* an employee of the university, am I?" she said. "Because you canceled my interview?"

"Where do you think you're going...?"

"To warn those kids you just narced on," Olivia said.

"As long as you're living in my house—and working at my school—you play by my *rules*, understood?" the dean said.

"Your rules are obsolete. Just like you."

Olivia walked across the street to the party. She could almost hear Dean Oldman shout behind her, "You're *grounded*, young lady!"

8.

She was a decade older than anybody else around. Students gave her perplexed looks, as if they could sense that she had long ago graduated from wild keggers to polite dinner gatherings. Or rather, from two-dollar Trader Joe's wine to five-dollar Trader Joe's wine.

"Hey everyone," Olivia shouted over the music, "you need to *clear out*."

Nobody paid attention. She turned off the sound system.

"Listen up!" Olivia said. "The cops are coming. You have to—"

Sirens outside. The police had already arrived.

"Give me your drinks," Olivia told the students, grabbing their beers. "I'm over twenty-one...you can't get in trouble if you're not holding them."

But she could only handle so many cups. The officers burst into the house, yelling "freeze!" and "ID cards out!" The students attempted to flee but, realizing they were surrounded, withdrew their identifications sullenly.

"Put down the booze, ma'am," an officer said to Olivia.

"I haven't been too young to drink since George W. Bush was president," she said. "It's flattering you think otherwise."

"Then you're under arrest," the officer said. "Contributing to the delinquency of minors."

"Wait...I didn't *buy* any of this alcohol for them."

"You don't need to purchase it, ma'am. By attending an event with underage consumption, you're de facto facilitating it."

"That makes *no* sense," Olivia said. "If I order chardonnay at a restaurant, and there are kids at the next table, I'm not—"

"Businesses are businesses," the officer said. "Law's the law. Come with us."

For the first time in her life, Olivia felt the cold snap of handcuffs. Police led her to the squad car. Dean Oldman watched from his driveway.

"This is *your* fault, you bloated asshole," Olivia shouted at her father.

"Pipe down," said the arresting officer, slamming the cruiser's backdoor. "You want an extra charge of disturbing the peace?"

9.

"Oh no, Professor Olivia," Pablo said, standing in a circle with Jackson, Ash, Meg, and Nikki.

"'Bloated' asshole is kind of fat shaming," Nikki said. "Why not just 'asshole'?"

"What's our teacher doing at a rager?" Ash said.

"She's totally DTF, bro," Jackson said. "Totally."

"Bro, I told you, we're woke male feminists now," Ash said. "We appreciate women for their intellectual contributions, not just by how 'DTF' they are. Be an *ally*, bro."

"I hate to say it, bro," Jackson said, "but you sound like a real puss lately."

"I'm calling you out!" Nikki said. "Pussies are

resilient and beautiful, and there's nothing wrong with them." She turned to the police. "Hey, dicks, you can't arrest her!"

"What's wrong with dicks?" Jackson said. "They're not resilient?"

A cop inspected the students' IDs—including Pablo's Deferred Action for Childhood Arrivals authorization card—and wrote tickets. "Here are your citations. You'll receive notice to appear in front of your campus disciplinary board."

"Busted, bro," Ash said.

"Weak sauce," Jackson concurred.

"Um, *obviously* you don't know who I am," Meg told the officer, "because I have the second most-watched YouTube influencer channel and I guarantee you that hashtag #FreeMeg will be trending in minutes. Do you want to explain *that* to your superiors?"

The cop handed Meg a citation. "Sure, it'll be just like the campaign for Nelson Mandela."

"Who's Nelson Mandela?" Meg said.

"Officer, excuse me?" Pablo said, still holding Ash's beer. "I wasn't drinking this."

The cop smirked. "You think I've never heard *that* bullshit line?"

"Please, my scholarship, my *citizen*ship...you don't understand."

The officer gave Pablo a ticket and moved to another group of students.

"This can't happen…" Pablo's expression was pure horror. "Can't happen. This can't, can't, can't, can't—" He was having a full-blown panic attack. "My life's over, my…over…life's…my…it's…"

Pablo fell to the ground, all but seizing. Nikki knelt and held his hand. "Hey, it's gonna be okay," she said. "I promise."

"Can't, can't, I can't, I…"

"We all saw you weren't drinking, and that's what we'll tell the disciplinary board. *We* broke the rules, not you. Sound good?"

"Uh," Jackson said, "do we have to?"

"*Yes*," Nikki said.

Pablo breathed easier. "Thank you so much."

He had found his friend group after all.

10.

Olivia sat inside a holding cell, furious but unable to rage-tweet because police had confiscated her iPhone. The world of twelve hours ago, in which she had expected to receive a tenure-track position—to receive a stable, self-sufficient life—seemed so far away. After a decade of missed opportunities, was reaching a single milestone of adulthood too much to ask?

I could be on a yacht in Ibiza right now... She kicked herself for the zillionth time. *Why did I dump Travis?*

A guard unlocked the sliding door. Dean Oldman had arrived to bring her home.

"I'll put bail on your tab," the dean said. "Was your little protest worth it?"

Olivia walked out of the cell without looking her father in the eyes. "The next protest," she said, "might not be so little."

CHAPTER THREE

11.

Bleary-eyed and seething, Olivia crossed the campus. She read the top headline printed on a stack of the *Logan Frost Daily Dispatch*: "Tuition Rising 35 Percent Next Semester."

No budget for teachers, though? She scoffed. *Yeah, right.*

Olivia walked past a group of students protesting a World War I-era statue. It depicted a former chemistry department head who had developed now-illegal weapons. Their signs read "NO STATUE FOR WAR CRIMINAL," "WRONG THEN, WRONG NOW," and "WARMONGER OFF CAMPUS."

It gave her an idea.

12.

Olivia trudged into the classroom, worn-out from two sleepless nights in a row. All of her students who had attended last night's party were just as exhausted, just as on edge.

"I can't do this today," Olivia said. "Or ever again. I just...hashtag #ICannot."

Nervous laughter from the students.

"Let's go outside. Field trip. Come on, everybody..." She led her class to the Main Hall steps. "Meg, take out your phone and begin a livestream."

"Yesterday I *couldn't* stream during class," Meg said.

"True," Olivia said, "but today you'll be streaming *me*."

"Umm, are you going to share makeup advice, Professor Olivia? Because TBQH, you look a little puffy this morning...from, uh, jail?"

"No, Meg," Olivia said, "I am not going to share makeup advice."

Meg pointed her phone at Olivia and tapped a red circle on the screen. "Heyyyyyyy, Meg Nation, we're coming to you *live* from campus and also from my professor's mental breakdown. So, here she is!"

Olivia breathed in, breathed out, and addressed the mass following.

"Fifty years ago, my father—back when he was cool—stood on these very steps, protesting against an unjust system that oppressed the youth," she said. "Thanks to him and millions of other young people who stood up for their own civil rights, society changed forever...or so we thought. The youth are *still* oppressed, except now the system's weapon is *debt*. Study after study proves that chronic anxiety shortens human lifespan by decades, and we're being diagnosed as far more anxious—and far more depressed—than any previous generation. Our loans are actually *killing* us."

Olivia sat on the granite stairs.

"We are going to stay here," she said, "until this university lowers tuition by half, cancels outstanding debt, and pays a living wage to *all* of its faculty. If you're with me, take a seat. If you want to stand up for something, let's sit down for it."

"And then do what...?" Jackson said.

"Nothing," Olivia said.

"What can *that* accomplish?"

"Everything."

13.

Linda knocked on Dean Oldman's office door.

"Mitchell?" she said. "You might want to see what your daughter is up to outside…"

Dean Oldman looked out the window. "I don't understand."

"They're holding a *sit-in*," Linda said. "Oh, I remember those. What fun!"

Fun? Dean Oldman thought. He recalled the blunt force trauma of the nightstick against his face, the days spent healing in a hospital bed as his mother and father—rest their souls—worried themselves sick over the possibility of brain damage. Did *that* stop the Vietnam War? Most certainly not. In fact, the hippies had *increased* popular support for the invasion, later studies proved, because average Americans hated them so very much. It would have ended sooner if he'd never protested at all. *The audacity…the gall.*

"I remember them not being particularly effective," Dean Oldman told Linda. "Let her sit. It won't make any difference."

14.

Nine hours passed. The students had not moved from the steps, many of them skipping other classes for this protest. They were struggling to remain awake. The brisk temperature dropped by the minute.

"Professor Olivia," said Pablo, "I don't think it's working."

"Has anybody even *noticed* us out here?" Nikki said.

"Yo, I'm starving," Ash said. "I thought this was a sit-in, not a hunger strike."

"If I don't get my whey protein," Jackson said, "I don't know *what* I'm capable of."

"Honestly, Professor," Meg said, "that livestream did *not* get many views, likes, or comments. I even lost a few thousand subscribers—which, humblebrag, never happens."

"I thought...with our message...don't people *care*?" Olivia punched her own thighs in frustration. "Let's all go home. We tried."

The students felt instant relief and left for their dorms. Only Caleb stayed behind in the dark. "Maybe we didn't try hard enough," he mused, gears turning in his head. Turning and grinding and cracking.

15.

Olivia unlocked her Prius in the faculty parking lot. A fellow professor in his thirties—dark hair cut in a neat low fade, both Japanese *kanji* and Hebrew lettering tattooed on his forearms—waved to her. "Hey, that sit-in was awesome," he said. "So righteous."

Stud alert, Olivia thought. *He probably won't invent a billion-dollar app, though.*

"We didn't make an impact at all…" Olivia shrugged. "I've seen you in the all-staff meetings, right? School of Communications?"

"Yeah…Benjy Li. I'm an adjunct, too. I've wanted to protest for *years* over how we're treated, but if you're the only one sticking your neck out…" He made a throat-slitting motion with his hand. "I guess I'm a coward."

"Well, apparently protesting—as popular as it is—doesn't, y'know, work."

"Only because your message was off," Benjy said. "It's Marketing 101. I mean, I *teach* Marketing 101, so…"

"How? Mansplain it to me, Benjy."

"An effective pressure campaign needs a national appeal, but you only made demands of *our* university. Why would students on every other campus support debt forgiveness here alone? You need to get them asking, 'What's in it for me?'"

"Huh...okay, that...actually makes a lot of sense." Olivia nodded. "Do you want to grab a drink? I'd like to talk more about 'what's in it for me.'"

16.

A framed photo of Theodore Kaczynski sat on the dorm room nightstand beside an open copy of *Industrial Society and Its Future*, also known as the Unabomber Manifesto.

"'In order to get our message before the public with some chance of making a lasting impression,'" Caleb recited, "'we've had to kill people.'"

With methodical precision, he taped a cardboard box. Sealed it tight. And carried it out of the dorm.

17.

Benjy brought a pair of copper mugs over to Olivia as classic rock played on the dive bar jukebox. *When did '90s jams become classic rock, anyway?* she wondered. *Do the kids still say "jams"?*

"A Moscow mule for you, comrade," Benjy said.

"I'll Venmo you," Olivia said. "When I have money in my account again."

"No need. My treat! Happy hour goes late here."

"A good feminist covers her half of a date."

"So," Benjy said, "I'm dating the boss's daughter now...dangerous!"

Olivia gave him a look. "*A* date, not dat*ing*...do people even use that word anymore?" She sighed. "Seems like 'swiping' has replaced it."

"Oh, I don't use any of those hookup apps," Benjy said. "If you'd told me in college that someday everyone would carry a magical fuck button in their pocket, the future would've sounded incredible. Even better than *The Jetsons*."

Olivia laughed.

"But nobody's *happy* using SwypeRite!" Benjy continued. "It's like toothpaste: If the store only has Crest and Colgate, making a decision is easy—they're both pretty good—but if you have countless options, then you just stand there in the grocery aisle, paralyzed by choice, because they all have pluses and minuses, so they all feel like a mistake. Like there's always something better."

"You aren't going to believe this," Olivia said, "but I dated the CEO during my sophomore year."

"The CEO of...SwypeRite?"

She opened Facebook on her phone and pulled up a 2003 photo—taken with a disposable Kodak camera, later scanned for #ThrowbackThursday—of her and Travis, cuddling in a dorm room. "He's, like, a billionaire now."

"Yeah, I know who he *is*," Benjy said. "Damn."

"I think about it a lot—what my life would've been if I'd stayed, if I were Mrs. Zachmann," Olivia said. "No debt, carefree, traveling the world...with that kind of money, you could solve any problem."

"Yeah," Benjy said, "but you'd have to be married to the kind of douchebag who creates a hookup app in the first place."

Olivia smirked and downed the Moscow mule in one gulp. "Want a second round?"

18.

The Main Hall, unlike most other buildings on campus—the library, the cafeteria, the auditorium—was not locked at night. Caleb entered the staff lounge and placed his box of mayhem on the table.

"And that's why they're called baby *boom*ers," he said to himself with a dark chuckle.

The door handle began to turn. Caleb ducked under the table; the package was still on top of it. Olivia and Benjy stumbled in, reeking of vodka.

"Sorry we have to do it here," Benjy said between wet, gingery kisses. "My roommate never leaves our studio."

Olivia snorted. "My roommate is my dad, so..."

"Let's please not talk about your dad right now?"

"Good call."

Benjy lifted Olivia onto the table. They ripped each other's clothes off. She stifled a laugh at his *Die Hard* logo-emblazoned boxer briefs.

"It's a pun," Benjy said.

"Right," Olivia said.

"Like an erection?"

"Yeah, dude, I get it." She licked his neck and traveled downward.

"It's also my favorite movie," Benjy said. "*Die Hard*, I mean, not *Like an Erection*—is there even a movie with that title? Sorry, I'm off-topic...ooh, that's nice."

A few feet below, Caleb tried to breathe without making a sound.

Olivia threw the box to the floor. "Let's clear this shit out of the way..."

Caleb's eyes widened with mortal fear as the box landed inches away from his face. No explosion. Pure luck. With the two professors distracted in naked passion, he snuck back into the hallway.

Tomorrow. The revolution would begin tomorrow.

CHAPTER FOUR

19.

Linda covered her mouth in shock at the sight of Olivia and Benjy entangled asleep on the table. The other tenured professors were right behind her.

"Oh...*oh* my," Linda said, wakening the two adjuncts, who—upon jolting to consciousness—searched for their underwear. "Pardon the, ah, interruption...it's time for our staff meeting, is all."

"A white lady with an Oriental man?" said P.O.W.G. #3. "Huh! Normally it's the other way around."

"'*Oriental*'?" Benjy said. "What century are you from?"

"He's only a halfie, looks like," said P.O.W.G. #2, pointing at Benjy's tattoos. "*Jew*panese...how exotic!"

"'*Exotic*'?" Benjy said. "I'm not a zoo attraction, man."

"Put on some clothes, you two," Linda said, "before the dean—"

Dean Oldman walked into the room. "All right, I know that reimbursement forms are nobody's favorite topic, but—"

His jaw dropped, brain struggling to process the raw data from his optic nerves, so unexpected was the sight.

"Dad...?" Olivia said groggily. "Oh shit."

"Sir," Benjy said, "I—I'm sorry, I—"

"You...and...my *daughter*...?" The dean's blood pressure spiked far above his physician-recommended upper limit. "You're fired."

"You don't *own* me," Olivia said. "You're not in charge of my *body*." She then puked all over the table, basting in a puddle of lime-scented bile.

"No," Dean Oldman said, "but I'm in charge of the furniture."

He averted his eyes as Olivia and Benjy put their clothes back on—and, in turning away, kicked Caleb's box on the ground. It smashed against the wall, activating the mechanism inside. KA-BOOOOOOOOOM.

20.

Panicked students ran out of the Main Hall, desperate to escape, tripping over and shoving one another. The therapy pig squealed and shat, lost in the pandemonium. Nikki, Pablo, Meg, Jackson, and Ash sheltered in a supply closet for the Department of Art and Design.

Meg took out her smartphone and began livestreaming. "OMG, you guys, I just want you to know that you're the best fans in the universe and, if this is goodbye, I love you so, so much. Also, my mom and dad, too."

"Put that thing *away*," Nikki whispered. "The attacker could hear you and come for us."

"You think it's a school shooter?" Ash said.

Jackson clenched his fists. "We'll *crush* him, bro."

"It's not a school shooter..." Caleb opened the closet door, speaking in a calm, matter-of-fact monotone. "It was a bomb. My bomb. It's lit, fam."

A hush fell over the small room.

"What...?" Ash said. "*Your* bomb?"

"You were all at that sit-in yesterday," Caleb said. "A waste of time and breath. People with power never give it up willingly; it has to be taken."

"What's *wrong* with you?" Nikki said.

"You want to *kill* people?" Meg said.

"Maybe we should go check if everyone's okay?" Pablo said.

"We *should* go check," Caleb said. "I want to see how I did."

21.

The smoke cleared inside of the staff lounge. Olivia tried to get her bearings despite the burning in her eyes and the ringing in her ears. All of the professors had survived. Minor injuries, it appeared—she would have called it a miracle, if she believed in them—except for P.O.W.G. #1, who lay in serious condition. Shrapnel from the bomb was stuck in his burnt face.

"Olivia, was this part of your…your *uprising*?" Dean Oldman said. "To lure us in here with that *scene* and then—"

"You're actually asking that?" Olivia said. "Whatever happened, it had *nothing* to do with me or my students."

Fire alarms and campus safety sirens blared through the window.

"Wrong again, Professor." Caleb stood in the

doorway with the other history students. "You wanted a revolution? Here it is."

"Caleb...?" Olivia put the puzzle pieces together in her still-disoriented mind: the kid's absolutist proclamations and insecure craving for respect, his attraction to the most extreme political voices...it wasn't just a testosterone-laden phase that she had seen—and seen pass—in countless freshmen; he was disturbed. "I didn't want to *blow people up*."

"Don't be naïve," Caleb said. "You teach the *history* of revolution. When has change—*true* change, not incremental, watered-down compromise—ever occurred without a body count?" Caleb turned to Meg. "Broadcast our manifesto."

Meg, scared but exhilarated—now *this* was viral content—pointed her phone at Caleb.

"Would Ted Kaczynski use a smartphone app?" Olivia asked Caleb. "Doesn't seem very Luddite-like."

"True," Caleb said, "but I'm willing to destroy the system with its own tools."

Meg gave Caleb a finger countdown of three...two...one. He faced the camera. "My fellow students—my brothers, my sisters, my acolytes—like you, we at Logan Frost University have traded our financial freedom for a worthless piece of paper," Caleb said. "Like you, we'll compete for scraps in a brutal, late-stage capitalist future. Like you, we're victims..." He gestured towards the dean and senior professors. "While *these* predators, our modern slave merchants, get filthy rich. That's why we're taking them hostage until we get *everything we want*."

Meg panned to the older faculty, who began shouting, crying, and holding hands.

"So, Professor," Caleb said to Olivia, "tell them what we want."

"I...I don't..." she stammered. "Nobody was supposed to..."

"Professor Olivia," Meg said, zooming in on her, "we've got half a million viewers already and it's going up fast. *Give* them something!"

Olivia's gut instinct was to denounce the act of violence and request help, to make it clear that Caleb did not speak on behalf of anyone but himself—that he was a lone wolf, a tempestuous lunatic—but a separate instinct tugged at her with greater force. As the old adage went: *Never let a good crisis go to waste.* This was a once-in-a-lifetime platform for everything that she believed in, for changing the world in positive, necessary ways. All she had to do was go along with Caleb's plan—the genie was out of the bottle—while keeping his vicious excesses in check.

"I don't believe in harming anyone," she said.

"These aren't the circumstances that I wanted to spread our message under...but history rarely provides ideal circumstances. Actually, history is *forged* by a lack of them. Most of you watching this were born at the dawn of the millennium, so you don't remember how life was before 9/11, before Iraq, before the recession, before the visible effects of climate change. We had so much *optimism*. We thought the world would just keep getting better and better. We listened to ska, for crying out loud. My first CD was *Tragic Kingdom*."

She smiled with nostalgia.

"And then we *became* a tragic kingdom," Olivia said. "Reality handed us twenty years of suffering, of decline. I don't know whom I pity more: older millennials like me for losing our hope...or younger ones like you for never hoping at all."

"Uh, excuse me?" Meg said. "We're Gen Z, technically."

Olivia paced back and forth, anger building up. "So, who took our hope away?" she said. "Who stole our futures, our careers, our affordable housing, our habitable Earth? *The baby boomers*. For all of human history, parents tried to leave a better world for their descendants—yet to the boomers, it's only about *themselves* and *their* quality of life. The wealthiest generation in history reliably votes to cut public schools, environmental regulations, and the social safety net..."

Caleb jumped in front of her. "While *funding* war after war for the sake of their oil investments," he interrupted. "No matter *how* many civilians and young soldiers die. No matter how many children are left *orphans*."

"I've got this, Caleb..." Olivia had already grown comfortable in the spotlight. "Boomers fetishize their own counter-cultural mythology while not living up to it. They said to 'question authority,' but call us uppity and fragile for questioning *their* authority. Old people don't know anything about this world anymore—they can barely send a text message or attach a photo without our help—but for some reason, they're still *ruling* the world...no wonder it's so cruel, toxic, and broken. We're changing that forever, today."

The students leaned forward. They had never heard a teacher get this impassioned.

"The boomers won't step aside, won't cede the tiniest bit of power, yet claim *we're* entitled," Olivia said. "They can't conceive of a universe in which they no longer call the shots, so they can't allow it to exist. They never wanted to leave a better planet for their children and grandchildren, or to leave anything at all—boomers killed the icebergs; millennials only killed iceberg lettuce—but *we're taking this planet back*. My students and I will hold these hostages until every single college loan is wiped clean. If you want them back, give us back our futures."

"Olivia, you can't do this," Dean Oldman said. Even in his radical days, he did not go so far as to kidnap anybody.

"You're in *my* house now, playing by *my* rules," Olivia snapped at him. "Youth power! Youth power!"

Her students chanted along: "*Youth power! Youth power!*"

CHAPTER FIVE

22.

In a high school hallway across town, a teenager named Alex pointed a Glock semiautomatic pistol at his own head. Instructors and classmates gave him a wide berth.

"See?" Alex said. "This is what *happens*. This is what you all *did* to me."

"They all did what...?" Agent Ariana Hermosa of the Federal Bureau of Investigation approached the teenager, carrying no weapon of her own.

"Who are you?" Alex said. "A cop?"

"I'm someone you can talk to...Alex, right? I work for the FBI. My name is Ariana."

"What...? Why is the *FBI* here?"

"The police didn't have a crisis negotiator available, Alex, so they reached out to us. And I'm reaching out to you. That's what I do: communicate. Help tense situations become calmer. Now…"

She said *communicate* and *become calmer* like instructions, punctuating each syllable at the most relaxing tempo. *Now* implanted it deeper, as she had learned—along with dozens of other inductions—at the American College of Hypnotherapy after completing undergrad in psychology at Logan Frost. An unorthodox background, but one that even initial skeptics at the Bureau's Critical Incident Response Group had to admit prepared her well for this high-stakes role.

"I don't have a firearm on me, promise," Hermosa said. "So, can we trust each other?"

"I…I wouldn't shoot you," Alex said, "or anyone else. I'm not *crazy*, just…"

"You're not crazy, Alex. I can see that. 'They' all did what to you?"

"The girls, they…I mean, I try to be a nice guy—I don't harass and I'm, like, a gentleman and stuff—but I still wound up an incel."

"'Incel'?"

"Involuntary celibate…we're kind of a political movement?" Alex's voice cracked. "Like, other guys can get girlfriends, you know? I don't have *that* bad of a personality. I can be sweet. But all of my promposals got turned down. The Friend Zone keeps sucking me back in!"

He pressed the gun harder against his forehead.

"Alex, I never dated in high school either," Hermosa said. "I got turned down so many times." She repeated Alex's own phrases back to him—*not crazy*, *turned down*—to build a subtle rapport, a subconscious wavelength. It was called mirroring. Hypnosis didn't lull people to sleep; it focused them.

"But you're so pretty!" Alex said.

"Thank you, Alex, that's very *sweet* of you. You are a *gentleman*. What a *nice guy*! But, see, in the early aughts, the LGBT community was far less accepted than we are today. A lot of us kept quiet about it. So, I couldn't find a girlfriend, just like you. I guess I was an 'incel,' too. You know what happened?"

"What?"

"I went to college...and people were different there," Hermosa said. "I even met my wife. It—helped —me—to—calm—down. *Now* she's having a baby next month."

"Really?" Alex said, facial muscles softening, blinks and swallows decreasing in frequency. "It's dope that all happened, that you found someone."

"It *is* dope." Hermosa laughed. "And if it all happened for me, do you think it could happen for you? Take a moment to imagine."

The young man's grip on the gun wavered. "Ariana...? I don't really want to die."

"It's so good to hear that, Alex."

"Thanks for listening to me." He lowered the gun, handed it to Hermosa, and gave her a hug. She returned the embrace and then slid Alex's Glock into her ankle holster.

Alex let out a shriek; pain surged through his wrists and forearms. His body slammed against a row of lockers with a hard, echoey thud. A gruff, mustachioed boomer—ex-military with plenty of old man strength—had snuck up from behind him.

"You brought a gun to school, punk," said Special Agent in Charge Liam Fitzgerald, handcuffing Alex. "Zero tolerance."

"*Ariana*...?" Alex said.

"I'm sorry, Alex, I meant every word," Hermosa said. "You'll find someone...really."

Fitzgerald rammed Alex face-first to the ground. "Don't talk to the perp like he's your *friend*, Hermosa," Fitzgerald said. "He's a worthless thug in a generation of worthless thugs. Ever hear of moral standards? We had 'em in my day."

"Go easier, boss—you'll kill him," Hermosa said as Alex whimpered.

"That so?" Fitzgerald grinned. "I thought he *wanted* to die?"

23.

"Whoa..." Meg stopped the manifesto livestream.

"You *killed* it, Professor Olivia," Jackson said.

"For real," Ash said. "That was bad*ass*."

The celebration was cut short by P.O.W.G. #1's howls of pain.

"Olivia, I know this is how you think you'll get your way," Dean Oldman said, "but if that man doesn't go to the ER—now—*you'll* go to *jail*. And I can't bail you out of a life sentence."

Olivia did not consider herself a criminal accomplice. She had known nothing about the bomb in advance. Her whole plan was to rein Caleb in; she was the voice of moderation. But the realization hit her: After that speech, in the eyes of the law—in the eyes of the world—she was the ringleader here. Nobody would believe that a student had taken charge. *For someone with a PhD*, she thought, *how am I so, so stupid?*

"Okay..." Olivia said. "Let's call an ambulance."

Caleb lifted his shirt to reveal a suicide vest. "No one is walking out of here unless *I* say so."

Everybody in the room screamed. He was even crazier than they had thought. Death wish crazy. Don't-care-who-I-take-with-me crazy.

"That's a shock," said P.O.W.G. #3. "You don't *look* Middle-Eastern."

Most of the baby boomers got a good, hard laugh out of that one.

"Whoa, dude, do you actually *know* any Muslims?" Olivia said. "Because the vast majority are peaceful and kind, just like any other group of humans. Maybe society wasn't as diverse in your day, but change is inevitable, so learn to adapt."

"Good job calling him out, Professor Olivia!" Nikki said.

"Yeah, who *talks* like that, except for Twitter Nazis?" Meg said.

"You fuckin' suck, bigot bro," Ash said. "That shit is wack."

P.O.W.G. #3 grimaced, arms crossed. "Oh, why can't you P.C. millennials take a joke?" he said, proceeding to mutter something about the First Amendment.

An amplified voice came from outside: "Students, this is campus safety. Release the hostages and exit the building, hands on your heads."

Caleb looked out the second-floor window. "*Back off*," he shouted. "We have more bombs!"

"*More* bombs?" Olivia said.

Linda cradled P.O.W.G. #1. "Please," she said to Caleb, "let them take him to the hospital."

"They do that in, like, every hostage movie," Nikki said. "As a sign of good faith? Seems like a solid move."

"Not in *Die Hard*," Benjy said. "But Hans Gruber agreed to bring a sofa down for the pregnant lady in Nakatomi Plaza, so...kind of the same thing?" P.O.W.G. #1 convulsed in Linda's arms. "Sorry, yeah, he needs medical attention."

"Let him go, Caleb," Olivia said.

"Fine," Caleb said. "But we're not trading any more leverage without results." He turned back towards the window, addressing the safety guards below. "We have one injured. Send EMTs up to get him. No surprises. And bring food...a week's worth."

"With vegan options!" Nikki added.

Olivia wondered if they could last for a week. The lobby had couches for sleeping, but where would they shower? What about clean clothes? Did the professors—and students, for that matter—require any medications? Caleb had planned for nothing; he certainly hadn't planned for tampons.

Benjy opened the staff lounge door. "I'm not a Hans Gruber myself," he said. "This is fucked-up. I refuse to take part. I'm out of here." He looked at Caleb. "You have any objection?"

"I won't stop you," Caleb said, "but history won't remember you. Only us."

"You're *leaving*...?" Olivia said to Benjy. "It was *your* idea to make this a 'national pressure campaign.'"

"Yeah, not to *kidnap* people," Benjy said. "This isn't how you win hearts and minds—it's how you'll lose *your* heart and *your* mind."

"You're un-fired," Dean Oldman said. "Take my daughter, please. She doesn't deserve you."

"*Quiet*, oppressor," Caleb said.

"No wonder you didn't protest 'for years,' wouldn't 'stick your neck out,'" Olivia told Benjy. "You *are* a coward. Why won't you stay and fight?"

"'Beware that, when fighting monsters,'" Benjy said, "'you yourself do not become one.'"

"Ooh..." Meg tweeted out the quote. "Harry Potter?"

"Nietzsche," Benjy said, shutting the door behind him.

It's nice you have the luxury of walking away, Olivia thought. *The second I leave, I'll get hauled off to some maximum security penitentiary.*

The only exit route was victory. She needed to know who would stick by her. "If anyone else wants to go, now's the time," Olivia said. "Pablo...?"

"I don't want other people to get hurt," Pablo said. "But the citation from that party the other night...if we could make it go away...I don't want to be deported. I don't even *know* anybody in Mexico!"

"Agreed on the citations," Nikki said.

"Those were fuckin' wack," Ash said.

"So wack, bro," Jackson said. "Let's make the cops stick 'em up their assholes."

"We'll...get those overturned, yes," Olivia said, relieved that her students were still committed to the cause. "Actually, who *wants* a drink? I have a bottle stashed in my classroom."

"First," Caleb said, "we need to make sure these oppressors aren't going anywhere..."

24.

He walked through the hallway to the Department of Art and Design supply closet and found a roll of twine on the shelf. "*Revolutionaries might consider favoring measures that tend to bind the world*," good ol' Mr. Kaczynski had written; Caleb would start by binding the professors' limbs.

Beside the twine sat a large-format paper cutter, built to slice a ream in a single drop. *Hmm*, Caleb thought. *That's interesting…*

Its blade was the right size for a guillotine.

25.

Police medics carried P.O.W.G. #1 across the quad on a stretcher, as EMTs were not authorized to enter hostage situations. The professor was conscious now, but lacked endurance for the officers' questions: "*Are the students armed?*" "*Are they a cult?*" "*Are they willing to kill for their beliefs?*"

Brevity had never been P.O.W.G. #1's forté as a lecturer of philosophy, but he tried to make himself clear. "Get the National Guard," he said. "Get the Marines. Get SEAL Team Six."

The professor gazed skyward as the morphine kicked in. A wave of opiate pleasure rolled over him. Even if he would need reconstructive plastic surgery, at least he was safe. Away from those fanatics, unlike the others. *Perhaps,* he thought, drifting far away, *there could even be a job opening for the deanship soon.*

26.

Fitzgerald grabbed Alex by the neck and shoved him into the FBI's jet-black SUV.

"This is some police brutality shit," Alex said, scooting as far across the backseat as he could, a bunny in the lion's den. "You're *sadistic*, man."

"Oh, I went easy, snowflake...I'm not cleaning teenage brains off my shoes right now, am I?" Fitzgerald shut the vehicle door, called in the all-clear Code Four over the interagency radio, and turned towards Hermosa. "Excellent work, Agent. What kind of mind control did you use to disarm him?"

Hermosa sighed. She hated working for this asshole, but—with her college loans—couldn't go back to treating cigarette addiction for twenty bucks per Groupon hypnotherapy session. "There's no such thing as mind control," she said. "All I do is help people align their outward behavior with their inner selves." She looked with pity at Alex inside of the SUV. "If there's any way to make a personal connection, I go for it...*mind*-handling them, not manhandling them."

"You're a goddamn miracle worker, Hermosa." Fitzgerald leaned in too close. "I don't know what we'd do without you..." He slid his hands down her hips. "What I'd do."

She twisted his fingers just enough to cause pain, but not enough to break them.

"Wasn't I making a 'personal connection'?" Fitzgerald winced. "You know, 'Go for it'?"

"I'm married, *boss*," Hermosa said. "To a woman?"

"If you ever wanna bring a man into the relationship..."

"You're disgusting." She released Fitzgerald's digits and stepped into the SUV driver's seat. "How was that shit *ever* acceptable?"

Fitzgerald shook the ache out of his hands. "Women used to find that kind of attention flattering, back when men were men."

As if summoned, Hermosa's wife sent a text message to the agent: *WTF is HAPPENING at our alma mater?!* The video of Olivia's speech was attached.

"Olivia fucking Oldman," Hermosa said aloud. "You haven't changed."

CHAPTER SIX

27.

"I call this Teacher's Little Helper," Olivia said, withdrawing a bottle of Svedka Citron from her desk. "I could get fired for sharing it with you, but I've broken plenty of HR policies today, so..."

She passed the bottle around the history classroom. All of the students took a gulp, except for Pablo.

"Professor Olivia," Pablo said, "I already got in trouble for drinking underage. My scholarsh—"

"It really doesn't matter anymore, bud," Olivia said. "We're outlaws now. *Vive la révolution.*"

Pablo took a nervous sip. His classmates cheered: "Pab-lo! Pab-lo!"

"Let's hear it for Professor Olivia, too," Ash said. "O-liv-i-a! O-liv-i-a!"

She blushed as the students chanted her name. She loved this feeling of bonding, of camaraderie. Even if the situation were to calm down soon—as she hoped—they would always cherish the happy memory of right now.

"Um, Professor?" Meg said. "Your video is getting comments from a *bunch* of TV news stations. Do you want to, like, talk to them?"

28.

A pair of cable news broadcasters introduced the next segment as a sensationalistic graphic warned of "UNDERGRAD UPRISING."

"They killed shopping malls, chain restaurants, taxis, newspapers, bar soap, home phones, and gluten," said one of the anchors, aged sixty-five. "Are millennials coming for *you* next?"

"Students today are more politically active than at any time since the 1960s and '70s," said the other anchor, aged twenty-seven. "Some call it a new civil rights movement."

"But are they going too far?" The old anchor pivoted to a different camera for a closeup. "At one campus, Logan Frost University, a student protest has become a full-blown hostage situation—with the dean and several professors being held against their will. The militants' leader, Olivia Oldman, joins us now by phone. Ms. Oldman, are you there?"

Olivia appeared on a split screen view, looking as jittery as she felt. A social media stream was one thing, but live TV was terrifying. At least Meg had put enough powder and setting spray on her to help keep the sweat at bay. "Thanks, um, for having me on," she said. "And I really wouldn't call us 'militant.'"

"But you *are* taking hostages until your demands are met?" said the old anchor.

"Nobody is in danger," Olivia said. "We actually released an injured staff member for medical treatment in order to show our commitment to resolving this situation with nonviolence."

"That staff member was 'injured' in a reported *explosion*, yes?"

"Uh...sort of?" Olivia cringed. It didn't sound great when framed that way.

"Can we see the other hostages," said the young anchor, "just to make sure they're safe and sound?"

Olivia walked to the staff lounge with her phone. The professors were tied on the floor. She knew the optics were horrible. "Safe and sound!" she chirped a little too optimistically. "We're not going to hurt them. All we want is for our generation's unjust, crippling debt to be wiped clean."

"Ms. Oldman," the old anchor said, "do you really believe the country will forgive *trillions* of dollars in loans?"

"Trillions is the *point*. Tuition has wildly outpaced inflation—just like housing, medical bills, childcare—and millennials can't afford to *live*."

Olivia recited statistic after statistic that she had written on a stack of index cards: Adjusted for inflation, millennials spent nearly 150 percent more on college, 75 percent more on healthcare, and 50 percent more on rent than baby boomers did at the same age; two-thirds of millennials had no retirement savings and suffered anxiety from college loans; the majority did not own homes even in their thirties; one in three still lived with parents; they had an individual net worth 34 percent below the historical average; and Social Security was predicted to run dry just as they would hit retirement age.

"We'll have to work until we're *ninety*," she said, "but the older generation, who already have more money than God, get free medicine *and* retirement from the government? Why can't we use the Social Security fund to make *us* socially secure now?"

"That argument is compelling," the young anchor said. "Heck, *my* student debt is out of control."

"But you knew what you were signing up for when you accepted those loans," the old anchor said. "Isn't taking money for a valuable degree and then refusing to pay it back just a form of theft?"

"*Are* degrees valuable anymore?" Olivia said. "That's what we're told, but wages flatlined while the cost of living exploded. A contract isn't valid if it's based on fraud, and that's exactly what our debt is. So, who *really* committed 'a form of theft'?"

"Touché," the old anchor said. "But why would the American people sympathize with kids who abduct their own teachers?"

"Because we *are* the American people," Olivia said. "And when you feel that you have a brighter future, then you won't burn the present to the ground."

"Is that a threat?"

"No...it's history."

29.

The students rushed into the staff lounge.

"You did so great, Professor Olivia," Pablo said, exhaling with relief as if he had held his breath during the entire segment. "I like how you mentioned 'our commitment to resolving this situation with nonviolence.'"

"You sounded woke AF," Nikki said with palpable pride. "I can't think of *anything* to call you out for!"

"Look, it's happening all over the country..." Meg showed realtime pics and videos—hashtagged #ImWithOlivia—of students at other universities taking over buildings.

"We did it," Caleb said. "We started the revolution."

"Hello, um, excuse me...?" interrupted P.O.W.G. #2, attempting to wave his bound arms. "I need to use the facilities."

"*Again*?" Caleb said. "It can wait."

"Someday, young man, you'll turn sixty, and your prostate won't be the same size it once was, and you'll realize that no, it *can't* wait."

"It's fine, Caleb," Olivia said. "We're following the Geneva Conventions here. Anybody else need a bathroom break?"

The professors all nodded.

"Okay, one at a time," Olivia said. "With a chaperone."

30.

Hermosa and Fitzgerald arrived at the Main Hall. The SWAT team now surrounding the perimeter checked their badges and logged their presence. Student onlookers stood behind yellow CAUTION tape, recording with their phones; some heckled millennial cops for picking the wrong side, for working against their own economic self-interest. News crews set up equipment, eager for a ratings bonanza.

"I haven't been back on this campus since 2006—it feels surreal," Hermosa said. "So many memories: cramming for finals in the library over there...walking across the quad to show off my new Razr flip phone..."

Fitzgerald ignored her reminiscences and approached a SWAT captain. "You haven't gone *in* yet?" he said. "What are you waiting for?"

"Security guards saw one of the hostage-takers wearing a suicide vest," the captain said. "We need to open a line of communication...and there's, uh, a pizza delivery for them."

Fitzgerald turned to Hermosa. "Sounds like you're up, Agent."

31.

P.O.W.G. #2 closed the stall door and let out a long, near-orgasmic sigh while urinating. Jackson, acting as chaperone, looked away to give him privacy. Did the metal walls need such wide cracks? What kind of voyeur designed these things?

"I understand why you're doing all of this," said the professor.

"Yeah?" Jackson said.

"You're young, you're angry, everybody is either totally good or totally evil...none of that is new. We thought *our* parents were heartless, behind the times. Cycle of life." The professor flushed the toilet and unlocked the stall door.

"I don't think y'all are heartless," Jackson said. "You just never faced what we've had to. Life was *easy* for you, so you've got no idea how—"

P.O.W.G. #2 flung the stall door open, holding the porcelain toilet lid. He tried to break it over Jackson's cranium.

"Whoa!" Jackson dodged the attack and hurled the professor into a wall-length mirror, shattering it into a thousand little shards.

A dead, broken body slid to the tiles below.

"Shit," Jackson said. "Shit. Shit. Shit. *Shit*."

CHAPTER SEVEN

32.

Olivia's phone rang. Her screen identified the caller as from the FBI; she assumed it wasn't a wrong number. "Hello?"

"Olivia! My name is Agent Hermosa...you know what? Call me Ariana. We're the same age. We actually overlapped at Logan Frost. And I have a stack of pizzas with your name on it."

"So, what, you're the hostage negotiator?" Olivia said.

"And I'm an advocate for you," Hermosa said.

Olivia knew that any negotiator worthy of the FBI would be a master of manipulation. She had to watch her own words very carefully. Was this person even telling the truth about having attended Logan Frost?

"You know our demands," Olivia said. "Debt relief for all, plus tenure-track for adjunct professors...oh, and I want my students' drinking citations thrown out, too." It sounded so trivial—silly—to her own ears. "I doubt you're authorized to make concessions on any of those."

"There are always options," Hermosa said. "Let's keep as many open as we can."

The friggin' FBI is taking me seriously, Olivia marveled. "I thought the U.S. government doesn't negotiate with terrorists?" she said.

"I don't believe you're a 'terrorist,'" Hermosa said. "I still have tons of student debt, too. I can't support your methods, but I do support your goal."

For a moment Olivia let herself believe that this plan might actually work, that she had indeed played her cards exactly right. "Tell me about the 'options.'"

"Can we do it face to face?" Hermosa said. "I mentioned the pizza, right?"

Olivia wondered if this was a trap. She checked the staff lounge refrigerator; the janitor had cleared it out the previous night. The vending machine was out of order. The barista had locked the espresso stand before fleeing. They needed food. Accepting it wouldn't obligate her to any deals. "No guns?" she said.

"No guns," Hermosa said.

Olivia paused to think it over. Was her guard already slipping? Or was this leadership? She saw no other viable alternative; none of them would want to butcher and eat the abandoned therapy pig, although she could envision Caleb putting its head on a stick like in *Lord of the Flies*.

"Fine," Olivia said. "Meet me in the lobby."

33.

"Any luck, Agent?" asked Fitzgerald, tapping his sidearm with impatience. "Or is it time to send in the cavalry?"

"Line of communication is open," Hermosa said, disconnecting her phone and relishing Fitzgerald's visible disappointment. Still, this would be a marathon, not a sprint. A marathon that could end in havoc.

"You've got one shot, Hermosa," Fitzgerald said. "After that it's my turn, and these snowflakes *will* get melted."

She walked towards the building.

34.

Jackson opened the staff lounge door with his bloody arm, shards of mirror still lodged inside of the flesh. "Uh, Professor Olivia...?"

The older faculty members gasped. This did not bode well for them.

"Jackson?!" Olivia said, recoiling at the sight of his injury. "What *happened* to you?"

He was on the verge on tears. "I think I messed up—like, real bad."

Olivia's expression conveyed both, *How bad is real bad?* and *I don't want to know.*

Jackson led Olivia and his classmates to the restroom. P.O.W.G. #2 lay dead and twisted on the floor. Meg and Nikki screamed. Pablo fell to his knees. Caleb stroked his chin, expressionless, analyzing.

"*Bro*," Ash said, "what did you *do*?"

"He came *at* me, bro," Jackson said. "I was trying to help that old bastard, and he turned on me. I had to defend myself...isn't that Bro Code?"

"I'm calling you out!" Nikki said. "'Bro Code' is just toxic masculinity, and you're a shining, shitty example of it."

"Oh my God," Olivia said, "the media will spin

this like we're ISIS. We'll be sent to Guantanamo Bay...is that still a thing?"

"Nobody says 'bae' anymore," Meg chimed in. "That went out with 'swag' and 'YOLO,' like, five years ago."

"I wasn't talking about *internet slang*, Meg..." Olivia dug her fingernails into her own forehead. Shit had officially gotten too real.

"Maybe he *deserved* to die for trying to hurt me?" Jackson said, growing frantic. "To hurt our *cause*...?"

"No, Jackson!" Olivia said. "We're *better* than that."

"Yeah, come on, amigo," Pablo said to Jackson. "That's just wron—"

"That's absolutely correct," Caleb said. "What did nonviolence get MLK and Bobby Kennedy? Bullets in the heads. What did turning the other cheek get Jesus? Nails in the hands. If you won't *kill* for your cause, then you'll *die* for it."

Jackson fist-pumped. "That's what I'm *sayin'*."

"Resist the dark side of the Force, bro," Ash said. "Don't go Kylo Ren on me."

"We didn't start this war on the boomers," Caleb said. "*They* started it on *us*. They drew first blood before we were even born."

"That's poetry to my ears, yo," Jackson said.

"*You're* the only one here with blood on your hands," Nikki said. "Literally."

Olivia groaned. This was hell, right? She was in hell now? They had all died and gone to the bad place for eternity? On the bright side, though, a student of hers had used "literally" in a proper context.

Her phone buzzed. Incoming call. FBI number.

"I'm in the lobby," Hermosa said on the other end. "Coming?"

"Give me a few minutes," Olivia said. "I'm...in the bathroom."

"TMI, girl."

Olivia hit disconnect and resisted the desire to yell her head off.

"Hide the body," she told the students. "I'll go buy us some time."

35.

"Delivered in thirty minutes or less," Hermosa said, her outstretched arms full of pizza boxes. "Tips welcome."

"I don't need your cutesy jokes." Olivia kept her own arms crossed, trying to conceal her panic—to put the dead man's face out of her distraught mind—and nodded towards a cube-shaped table by the couches. "I need loans paid off for millions of us. So give me a dollar amount."

"Before I can help you, Olivia, I need you to help me. Are the hostages unharmed?"

"Yes, I've said this over and over." Olivia began to sweat; she hated lying. "We care about justice, not some...*body count*." Never mind that Caleb had declared it necessary. "Paging Doctor Obvious."

Hermosa set the pizzas on the table, listening closely. "I'm *somebody* who *cares* about *justice* too, *obvious*ly," she said. "We're on the same *page*, *count* on it. So can we get—this—over—with? Now..."

Alarm bells went off inside Olivia's head. The FBI agent's phrasing was odd, its tempo unnatural, yet so familiar. "Are...you trying to use *mirroring* on me?" Olivia said. "Neurolinguistic programming?"

Hermosa's eyes widened as if Olivia had punched her in the gut. "What's, um, that...?"

"Subtly working *my* language into *your* responses? Planting a sly behavioral suggestion?" Olivia felt the old rush of competition; she had just thrown a strikeout against the designated hitter with bases loaded. "One of the few perks of teaching here is that I can audit the psychology courses."

Hermosa laughed. Game saw game. "You got me, Olivia. That's...never happened in my career."

"No more Jedi mind tricks," Olivia said. "Are you meeting our demands or not?"

"Look, the university's board of trustees has informed the FBI that, if you surrender now, they can forget about this, just like they forgot about your father's civil disobedience in the 1960s. Maybe you can even be dean someday like him."

Olivia wanted to accept the pardon, but knew that the dead professor upstairs made it a pipe dream. She'd spend the rest of her life in jail—the good years, anyway—but at least she could save countless others from debtor's prison in the meantime.

"Maybe you perform a few months of community service," Hermosa continued. "A light slap on the wrist. Not a bad deal, right?"

"I'm here to change the world," Olivia said. "I don't care how sore my wrist gets. You're a negotiator? Then negotiate us a better deal, because your opening offer sucks a bag of dicks."

Hermosa tossed a few packets of red pepper, thyme, and parmesan onto the pizza boxes. "Don't let this be your last meal, Olivia...my people are *not* messing around."

"Neither are mine."

CHAPTER EIGHT

36.

"COED CARNAGE," flashed the cable news graphic. Footage played of police immobilizing students across the country with pepper spray and rubber bullets; masked young people attacking AARP offices, burning down a gated retirement community, and hitting baby boomer golfers with their own clubs; and septuagenarian Hell's Angels attacking random millennials with bike chains and brass knuckles as generational payback.

"The protests at Logan Frost University have lit a fire that's spreading far and wide," the young anchor said. "Students at more than *forty* colleges nationwide have occupied buildings, all making the same demand for student loan forgiveness."

"Financial stocks are plummeting on Wall Street in response," said the old anchor. "Pressure is mounting on Congress to act. We're joined now by Brenda Jane Ellis, chairwoman of the Senate Banking Committee. Senator, welcome to the program. What's your reaction to this perilous situation?"

The senator, wearing a red pantsuit with a U.S. flag pin attached to the lapel, appeared on-screen from a balcony in the white-marbled rotunda of the Russell Senate Office Building.

"Perilous, indeed," Ellis said. "Not only for all of those poor, captive professors, but for our captive nation. If radical, unhinged demonstrators can intimidate taxpayers into loosening up our federal purse strings, what's next? Targeted assassinations? Hijacked airplanes flying into skyscrapers?"

"Senator, with all due respect," the young anchor said, "can you really compare a college sit-in—even one with some hostages, even one that's inspired a few small-scale acts of violence—to *9/11*?"

"Appeasement never works," Ellis said. "It only encourages more aggression. If you were a few years older and had seen more history, you would understand that."

"What about the 2008 and 2009 bailouts?" the old anchor said. "We gave struggling banks a trillion dollars, so why not struggling students?"

"A completely different situation," Ellis said. "If the financial sector had collapsed, society as we know it would be over. We're talking about a crisis."

"It's *not* a crisis that millennials are going childless because they can't afford to start families?" the young anchor said, growing agitated, hinting at a source of personal distress.

The senator laughed; it was time for hardball. "If you want more babies," Ellis said, jabbing her index finger at the camera, "the solution is to overturn *Roe v. Wade*, not to approve yet another handout for twentysomething leeches who lack the drive and desire to find work. When will you people realize that all of your misery is your own damn fault, not ours?"

The wide-eyed young anchor silently mouthed, "*Wow*."

"Senator," the old anchor said, "it doesn't sound like you hold today's youth in high regard."

"You mean the spoiled, failure-to-launch brats who never got out of their parents' basements?" Ellis said. "Always asking what their country can do for them, not the other way around? *Gimme this, gimme that*, freebie after freebie...maybe if they didn't spend a thousand dollars on the latest iPhone each year—because delayed gratification is a foreign concept—they'd have more savings and fewer complaints?"

The old anchor couldn't hide an ear-to-ear smirk. "I have to say, Senator, you described my son to a T. I love him, I do, but *when* can I stop chipping in for his rent? He claims to have no money, but then I see 'Pornography Hub Premium' listed on the credit card statements that I pay for him."

The young anchor looked appalled by the embarrassing disclosure. What kind of mockery would the son receive on social media within moments? Since boomers grew up without the internet, did they not comprehend how deep its scars could go?

"Indeed," Ellis said. "But if the free-speech-hating, socialist millennials had it their way, all such criticism of them would be illegal. We should raise the voting age to *forty*; Real America cannot allow this unstable, ungrateful, unpatriotic generation to become a majority of the electorate."

"You certainly don't seem to *want* our votes," the young anchor said.

"I'll let you in on a little secret," Ellis said. "You know why the average age of U.S. senators is sixty-one, not twenty-one? *Because the youth vote doesn't matter.* I'll say it! Has *never* mattered, *will* never matter."

"Strong words," the old anchor said. "Thank you, Senator."

"Fuck you, Senator," the young anchor said. "Youth power!"

The news feed cut to an incredibly abrupt commercial break.

37.

Hermosa had returned to the quad rattled by Olivia's shrewdness. It should have been easier to outmaneuver someone who'd cruised to straight As by virtue of her last name.

"What do you *mean*, 'No deal'?" Fitzgerald said. "You know who turns down a *full goddamn pardon* for cooperation? Zealots. Mafia. 'Sovereign citizens.' Give millennials an inch and they'll take a mile. They're the end of our civilization, mark my words!"

"Those students' frustrations are legitimate," Hermosa said, "just not their actions."

"No one who holds senior citizens for ransom has *any* legitimacy. Are you a federal agent or not? Is this entire country going insane?"

Hermosa was so sick of Fitzgerald bashing her generation. Could he not see that it's self-defeating to oppose the youth—spitting into the wind—because sooner or later they'll grow up to replace you, to replace your ideas? Hermosa began to feel a weird, grudging respect for Olivia, who was a royal pain in the ass but at least believed in something bigger than herself...

Or did she?

"We need to make a better offer," Hermosa said. "Monetary."

"Oh, *brilliant* idea," Fitzgerald sneered. "Let's clear out Fort Knox and back the truck up for these Che Guevara cosplayers."

"Not money for *them*...for her."

Fitzgerald leaned in, intrigued.

38.

The students, ravenous by now, crammed slice after slice of pizza into their faces. Vegan Nikki made a onetime exception for dairy; ketogenic Adonises Jackson and Ash made a onetime exception for refined carbohydrates.

"Maybe we should take some pizza upstairs," Pablo said. "For the professors?"

"After seventy years of abundance," Caleb said, "they can starve for one night."

"Geneva Conventions, remember?" Olivia told Caleb. "That's very thoughtful, Pablo."

Pablo carried a pizza box to the staff lounge, feeding the hostages by hand since theirs were tied. It felt strangely parental, as if he were a mother bird, albeit one with chicks quadruple its age.

"Thank you, young man," Linda said after Pablo had wiped her mouth with a napkin. "I've always believed that goodhearted people outnumber the bad."

"Generally I'm for the border wall, but we should let you stay," said P.O.W.G. #3. "Mexico *did* send us their best for once—and, hell, you even speak English pretty good!"

Linda shot her colleague a sharp, disapproving glare.

"Um, thanks..." Pablo said. "It's 'pretty well,' though."

"Yes, you're a good kid, we can tell," Dean Oldman said. "You'll let us go, won't you? While the others aren't here? Guaranteed *summa cum laude*!"

Pablo glanced at the impromptu security camera that Caleb had set up via iPhone video call. It would be too risky to free them. And Caleb scared the living crap out of him. "I wish I could, Mr. Dean, sir, but...cheese or pepperoni?"

Out the window, Pablo saw Hermosa return to the Main Hall.

39.

"Who the fuck are you?" Caleb said as the doors opened.

"Mind your mouth, Caleb—she's FBI," Olivia said, hoping it would sound like a chiding of impoliteness to Hermosa and a warning against self-incrimination to the students.

"Oh, I'm just a proud alum..." Hermosa walked into the lobby. "Taking a stroll down memory lane. How's the pizza?"

"This pizza is *bomb*, yo," Jackson said.

Olivia and Hermosa both looked confused. "Like 'da bomb'?" they asked in unison, children of the '90s.

"Yeah, not bomb like *bad*...bomb like dope," Ash explained. "So the pizza is bomb, but Caleb's actual bomb is wack."

Olivia changed the subject. "Back so soon?" she asked Hermosa. "I thought I told you to get me a better offer."

"I did get *you* one, Olivia," Hermosa said. "Can we talk alone?"

"Whatever you have to say, you can share it with all of us."

"This is awkward, but…Olivia, the government was never going to pay a full ransom—one-tenth of the economy—but what if we could wipe out *your* student debt? This very minute?"

"Mine…?" Olivia gulped. "All seventy thousand?"

"Plus the interest," Hermosa said. "My boss just had the funds approved, and he is *not* an easy man to convince."

"But…what about my students?" Olivia looked at Ash, Jackson, Nikki, Meg, and Caleb, their mouths agape. "*All* of the students in the country?"

"Your students won't face prosecution," Hermosa said, poker-faced. "No more offers are coming, so take it or leave it. I'm offering you a way out, Olivia, the *only* way out."

Olivia felt dizzy. She balanced herself against the wall, imagining a life without debt. Her own place. Travel. Clothes that weren't from half a decade ago. Fun. Ease. If, that is, she could live with herself. The escape route from her personal hell would leave millions stuck in theirs. How many years of grad school could Judas have paid off with thirty pieces of silver?

"It's okay, Professor Olivia," Nikki said. "Gotta do what's right for you."

"Yeah, we'd totally understand," Ash said. "Who *wouldn't* take that cash?"

"Get it, get it," Meg said.

Caleb, however, shook his head. He peered at Olivia with scathing, accusatory eyes.

"I...I..." She took a deep breath. It was so tantalizing. But if she were to expunge her negative net worth this way, she would never acquire a positive self-worth. She had already spent years dwelling on her mistakes—drowning in them—and couldn't swallow another drop of guilt. "*Can't.* Hashtag #ICannot."

Hermosa sighed. "Please don't make this mistake," she said. "Don't let the perfect be the enemy of the good."

"You're trying to divide us, but *nothing* can break this movement apart." Olivia regained her balance and stood tall, wagging a finger in Hermosa's face. "You might not feel solidarity with our generation, bitch, but *I* do."

"Is your favorite meal the hand that feeds?"

"Ugh, you sound exactly like my stupid dad."

"Oh, that's rich..." Hermosa's nostrils flared. "You don't seem to remember me from college, but I sure as hell remember you, Olivia, because our professor wouldn't *dare* give you a bad grade. The rest of us had to *work* for it."

"I got *no* favors," Olivia said. "I had to work *twice* as hard as my classmates."

"You got to play life on easy mode..." Hermosa turned away; she had never left a negotiation before. "You still can't see it."

40.

Fitzgerald was right, Hermosa thought, stomping down the front steps. *She is a fucking zealot. If anybody gets killed tonight, then it's on her, not me.*

It was a mistake to walk off like this, Hermosa knew. A negotiator can never give up on hostages—she *wasn't* giving up—but Olivia was only tolerable in microscopic doses.

"'No deal' again?" Fitzgerald said. "Pity, pity, pity...now we do it my way."

"Hey, feds..." The SWAT captain walked Benjy over to them. "Professor Li here mighta pinpointed the terrorist leader's weak spot."

"You know Olivia?" Hermosa asked Benjy.

"Yeah, hi, kind of..." Benjy lifted his phone; its

Facebook app loaded a dorm room photo from 2003. "But this guy knows her better."

Her and Travis Zachmann? Hermosa thought. *I am so behind on campus gossip.*

CHAPTER NINE

41.

Senator Ellis sat at her expansive mahogany desk in the Russell Senate Office Building, smoking a cigar, drinking from a tumbler of scotch, and writing a bill to withhold federal funds from states that legalize recreational marijuana. God's kingdom of America was not going to become a slothful nation of cannabinoid dependence and decadence on her watch. Whatever happened to "*just say no*"? Whatever happened to traditional family values?

"Senator...?" Her top aide opened the door.

"I'm busy," Ellis said. "Fuck off, Jew Boy." It was an affectionate nickname that she had for him; she had a lot of affectionate nicknames, although the recipients never seemed to adopt them.

"Yes, Senator," said the aide. "But you might want to see these approval numbers after your latest TV interview."

Ellis looked up from her paperwork. The aide placed a chart in front of her with a sharply declining line. "Christ almighty," she said. "That bad, huh?"

"The appearance was, uh, a *little* over the top, Senator? Youth voter registration is higher than anticipated this cycle. And you've alienated, um, all of them."

"Midterms are three weeks away..." Ellis pounded on the desk. "Well, when you shit the bed, the only thing left to do is clean your own damned mess."

"Is that a metaphor, or...?"

"Get me on a helicopter."

42.

Olivia's phone buzzed. A Palo Alto number. Travis's profile pic—one of the most well-known faces in the world—flashed on her screen.

"Oh my God..." She lost her breath, overloaded with conflicting emotions. This was the most insane day of her life. "Why would he...what would we even...okay, okay, just, yes, *try*." She accepted the call. "Um, Travis?"

"Hey babe," Travis said. "Can I still call you 'babe,' babe?"

"Nobody's called me that in fifteen years...but I guess so?"

"Cool. So anyway, babe, I heard you were on the news? And I wanted to make sure everything's chill?"

"I'm...shocked you still care."

"Actually, on the down-low, this *super* sexy-sounding CIA agent who says she went to Logan Frost with us, which is *so* cool—I wonder how many bad guys she's killed undercover on special ops missions, like, '*KAPOW, KAPOW, KAPOW*, fuck you, evildoers'?—wanted me to ring you up, but you didn't hear that from me, babe."

"Right," Olivia said.

43.

Agent Hermosa, eavesdropping on the call from the FBI's mobile command center, facepalmed and groaned.

How did such a douchebag get so, so rich? she wondered.

44.

"So look, babe," Travis told Olivia, "we've gotta get you out of there before the deep state's drones and killer robots bust in, all, 'KABLAM! You're dead! KABLAM! *You're* dead! Resistance is futile, mofos!'"

"Is...that what the 'super sexy-sounding CIA agent' *said* would happen?" Olivia asked.

"She *implied* it. And gave me your bank routing number. So I'mma donate a couple mil to pay for whatever it is you're protesting about, cool? Vaccine autism awareness or something?"

"Student loan forgiveness," Olivia said. "Good guess, though?"

"Nice," Travis said. "Not my problem, obv—I'm balls deep in cash, babe—but nice."

Olivia could remember why their relationship had not worked out; Travis didn't excel in stimulating conversation. Her mind drifted to Benjy.

"That's amazingly generous, Travis," she said, "but we need two *trillion*, not two million."

"Well, I'm not *that* balls deep in cash, babe...maybe in a few years?" Travis said. "But even with just two mil, your face goes on the cover of *TIME*, Emma Watson plays you in the HBO miniseries—or Emma Stone, or Emma Roberts, or *some* Emma—plus everybody calls you a hero...and you *are* a hero, babe. To me."

"Why are you doing this?" Olivia said. "I'm almost surprised you even remember dating me."

"I owe *everything* to you," Travis said. "Shit, why do you think I *created* SwypeRite? It was so I could move on from you—by having a bunch of meaningless sex with complete strangers who couldn't hurt me."

"So...if we'd stayed together...you wouldn't even *be* a billionaire?"

"Yo, girl, that's what I'm *sayin'*."

Olivia realized that all of the countless hours she had spent wondering *what if...* were a waste of time. She felt a decade and a half of regret seep out of her soul. Why had she been so shallow and materialistic, anyway?

"You know what, Travis?" Olivia said. "Keep the money. Hermosa is using you to control me—just like my dad wants to control me, just like the loan consolidators want to control me—but *I'm* in charge now."

"I believe in you, babe," Travis said. "Because *you* believe in you, and that's what it's all about. You've got the skills to pay the billlllllls."

"Bye, Travis. It was weirdly nice talking again."

45.

Hermosa threw her phone down to the grass in frustration as the sky darkened above. Travis had forgotten to mention, as they'd discussed, that the two million dollars—a tax write-off for him—would cover all of Olivia's *pupils'* debts, a far less Faustian-sounding offer than the previous one.

"Why is he so stupid?" Hermosa said. "Why is she so stubborn?"

"I'm beginning to wonder if the problem is *her* or *you*," Fitzgerald said. "Not seeing your best work today, Hermosa. Maybe, on some level, you *want* this rebellion to succeed? Maybe you have too much of a stake in it?" He patted his pistol again. "Because otherwise, you'd want to *end* it." Fitzgerald's phone rang; he picked up. "Ma'am...? It's an honor, but...*now?* Are you shitting me...? Yes, of course we'll be ready in...twenty *minutes?!*"

Hermosa had never heard such fretful deference in her boss's voice. "What was *that?*" she asked after he disconnected.

"Hell freezing over," Fitzgerald said.

46.

Feeling both wired and exhausted, Olivia paced around her desk. The students sat at theirs. "I've thought it over...we have to tell the authorities about the dead professor in the bathroom," she said. "If we're honest—it was unintentional—then we'll be in way less trouble than if they find out later."

"Maybe *you'll* be in less trouble," Jackson said. "But *I'll* still go to jail for manslaughter or some shit."

"Bro, bro, bro..." Ash said. "Maybe you should've thought about that before you straight-up *killed* a dude?"

"Harsh, bro."

"Snitches get stitches," Meg said, not looking up from her phone, "but apathy is even less popular. And that would poison my brand."

Nikki gazed out the window at the FBI and SWAT presence. "We'll be lucky if stitches are all we get by the time this is over."

"I don't want anyone else to die," Pablo said, "so if telling the truth is less dangerous..."

"We have to protect Jackson," Caleb said. "He's one of us. We volunteer nothing."

"Sweet," Jackson said. "You're more of a bro than my *actual* so-called bro." He exchanged a dirty look with Ash.

"Besides," Caleb said, "if the feds learn about our neutralized oppressor, they'll come after us guns blazing..." He gestured towards his suicide vest. "*This* might not even deter them anymore."

Olivia put her head in her hands; it seemed to weigh a thousand pounds. The maniacal kid was going to get them all killed. "Maybe you could *not* wear dynamite around everywhere?" she said. "We need to *de*escalate here."

"Why? Because you say so? Because you're in charge? Because you're *older*?"

"Yes, Caleb, it's called *in loco parentis*. I'm responsible for you." Olivia paused. "And that FBI agent *is* trying her damndest...maybe her next offer will be good enough to live with."

"'Good enough'?" Caleb scoffed. "You're just like the rest of this corrupt, decrepit country."

"I get what Caleb's saying," Meg said, still facedown in the glow of the endless scroll. "Like, can someone over thirty really understand us? No offense, Professor, it's just...that's super old. Like, if you joined a social network that I'm on, I'd wonder if it was still cool."

"We know Professor Olivia's got our backs," Nikki said. "So what if she's thirty? We're all adults here. That's the whole *point*."

"Yeah, I trust Professor Olivia," Pablo said.

"We don't need a white-haired savior—we need to liberate ourselves," Jackson said. "I'm with Caleb."

It's only a couple gray hairs, jerk, Olivia thought. *Why is coloring so expensive, anyway?*

"You're just looking out for yourself, bro," Ash said. "The cause is about *all* of us, not only your ass."

"Bro," Jackson said, "I'm picking up some real un-chill vibes from you."

"I'm *not* feelin' chill, bro. None of this feels chill at all."

"You wanna *do* something about it? Come at me, bro."

"*You* come at *me*," Ash said as the other students traded uneasy glances.

"Bro, it's *on*..." Jackson threw the first punch. Ash then landed a roundhouse against Jackson's cheek. They both went to the ground, wrestling for dominance like two boys obsessed with Ultimate Fighting Championship.

"*Stop* it, you meatheads," Olivia shouted. Her phone buzzed. FBI. She answered the call. "What do you want now?"

"Take this meeting," Hermosa said. "Trust me."

47.

The helicopter landed on the quad, its rotor downwash blowing cherry blossom branches in all directions. From the lobby, Olivia watched Senator Ellis and an aide disembark, trade handshakes with the FBI agents, and walk towards the Main Hall with Hermosa. It was so odd to see the high-ranking lawmaker in the flesh, caked in makeup for the TV cameras everywhere. *Like a Madame Tussauds wax figure come to life,* Olivia thought.

"Olivia," Hermosa said as the doors opened, "this is Senator Brenda Jane Ellis."

"Oh, I know who she is," Olivia said. "I just don't know what she's doing here."

"You must think I'm a hardhearted, hard-ass hardliner, Ms. Oldman," Ellis said. "But getting elected to the upper chamber takes some level of pragmatism. As much as I've opposed it, student debt forgiveness *is* polling well. And I'll admit, something is very wrong if a B.A. or even an M.A. is no longer a ticket into the middle class. So I have a compromise that should satisfy you as much as my first husband satisfied me once, forty-five years ago."

"There are sit-ins all over the country," Olivia

said. "Why are you coming *here* with a 'compromise'?"

"You're the founder of this student movement, the face of it—they'll *listen* to you," Ellis said. "Right now you might be even more powerful than I am. Ain't that just a kick in the crotch?"

"In person," Hermosa said, "you're *really* not like you are on television, Senator."

"So...we won?" Olivia said. "All of the student debt is gone now?"

"Slow your roll," Ellis said. "Two trillion is an enormous slice of GDP. Wiping it clean overnight will cause another recession—perhaps another Great Depression—which wouldn't make life any easier for you millennials."

"Okay, then," Olivia said, "what *would* make our lives 'easier,' according to you?"

"What if the price of a diploma were tied to the earnings made with it?" Ellis said. "Students would pay nothing upfront; instead they'd owe five to ten percent of their wages—on a sliding scale—for five to ten years, minus what graduates have already paid." She paused. "Same way I owe my bookie."

"Kind of like a tax?" Olivia said.

"Kind of like a tax." Ellis grimaced. "But let's

not *call* it that, because I want another term in office."

Olivia thought it over. Was it ideal? Not quite. But it was *a* deal, a vastly better one than the current system. "That...actually sounds pretty reasonable," Olivia said. "How do I know you'll be able to get it passed, though?"

"Because otherwise, Ms. Oldman," Ellis said, "I wouldn't give you the time of day. I've been wrangling votes—herding cats, we call it on the Hill—since before you were born."

The aide presented Olivia with a statement to sign, urging an end to the nationwide protests.

"I also want the pardons for my students," Olivia said.

"No shit," Ellis said. "It's in there, assuming they aren't murderers yet."

"Always read the fine print..." Olivia forced a smile, but felt sick.

"Then we have a deal?" Hermosa said.

Olivia signed the document, her shame mixing with a cascade of endorphins.

"Maybe you millennials aren't so goddamn unreasonable after all," Ellis said.

"When an entire generation feels the same way," Olivia said, "there's a *reason* for it."

"Put that slogan on a bumper sticker and run for office. You're a natural, sugar."

Hermosa clapped her hands. This was a negotiation for the history books. "Olivia, I take back what I said before. You *can* make the hard decisions. And the right ones."

"It...does feel right," Olivia said, "doesn't it?"

"No!" Caleb lurked in the shadows. "Professor, these people are *vampires* who've feasted on our lifeblood. Ten *percent* for ten *years*? College should be *free*."

Olivia jumped, goosebumps rising up her arms. How long had Caleb been eavesdropping? Why was everything he did so creepy? She could not let him torpedo this resolution.

"Maybe it will be free someday," Olivia said, more aware than ever of Caleb's suicide vest. "Let's celebrate this victory today and start working on the next victory tomorrow—like how civil unions led to gay marriage, how Obamacare led to calls for single-payer..." She glanced at Hermosa. "A smart woman once told me, 'Don't let the perfect be the enemy of the good.'"

Olivia noticed a small cardboard box in Caleb's hand. He had dropped similar ones behind him like a breadcrumb trail, all the way up the stairs. She shuddered to think what was inside.

"I'm not meeting in the middle—I'm ridding the world of *pestilence*," Caleb said, a wildfire in his eyes. "It's like Mr. Kaczynski wrote: 'By forcing a long series of compromises on the weaker man, the powerful one eventually gets all of his land... Revolution is much easier than reform.'"

"Caleb, that's enough!" Olivia said. "If I keep turning down every offer, we'll end up with nothing. Let's take *most* of what we want."

"If you were dying from an infection, would you only take 'most of' your antibiotics?" Caleb said. "No, you'd wipe out the pox! And *that's* what the baby boomers are."

"There are kids—people—on campuses all over this country *depending* on us right now to make that deal, Caleb. Purity isn't a policy."

"Didn't you hear Ellis say that we can crash the global economy?" He juggled the box. "We hold all of the cards here. They're *scared* of us; they've always *been* scared of us. You think it's a coincidence that the U.S. president has to be over thirty-five? They'll never let the youth run this country; bigotry against us is embedded in the Constitution. Maybe we *should* crash everything as payback for all they've stolen."

"Do you even remember the recession?" Olivia said. "Weren't you, like, ten at the time? People went from upper middle class to 'tent cities' in the blink of an eye. Good jobs became unpaid internships. The suicide rate skyrocketed. We cannot go back to that. Ever."

"Oh, I remember the recession, Professor." Caleb glowered. "The bank took our house—Mom couldn't afford the mortgage when the baby boomers sent Dad to die in Iraq—but did *we* get a bailout? No! Child services put me in foster care with complete strangers so I wouldn't grow up homeless, and then Mom killed herself. The most evil generation in history stole my *family*."

Olivia was stunned. Her student's fury made a kind of sense now. "Caleb, I'm so sorry you went through that," she said. "I know what it feels like to lose a parent."

"You don't know *anything* about me."

"I do. I lost my mother, too. From cancer. It wasn't fair. It made me angry. It made me lash out. It's the worst thing in the world. Losing *two* parents must be—" Olivia looked around the room. "Wait...where did Hermosa go?"

CHAPTER TEN

48.

Agent Hermosa looked through door after door, searching for the captive professors. Olivia's hostage video and cable news appearance had shown them in the staff lounge. Hermosa knew it was located somewhere at the far end of the hallway. She glanced in the history classroom, saw the students inside, and—heart pounding in her chest—ducked past it, careful not to step on the scattered little boxes.

Get out of here alive, Ariana, she told herself. *And then go back to curing nicotine addiction on Groupon.*

A few doors down, Hermosa found the faculty. "FBI," she said, twisting the knob and kicking the door open in case any hostage-takers were on the other side. Only immobilized senior citizens greeted her.

"Oh, thank God," Dean Oldman said. "We're rescued."

"I can't get you all out of here by myself..." Hermosa withdrew the radio transceiver from her kit belt. "But I'll let my team know your whereabouts and conditions. Are you hurt?"

"One of us is missing," Linda said. "He went to the restroom hours ago and never came back. Maybe he escaped?"

Hermosa felt a sinking sensation in her guts. "The only staff to leave were Professor Li and your colleague who needed a medical evacuation," she said. "I'll check the bathrooms. In the meantime, stay calm. Olivia has agreed to a peaceful solution."

"I know my daughter, Agent," Dean Oldman said. "And I've watched that...*Caleb* kid. She thinks she has a handle on this, but she absolutely does not."

49.

Pieces of mirror lay jagged across the floor. Blood had been wiped away. A rush job, barely a coverup to trained eyes. Hermosa checked the urinal area—nothing—and then the stalls one by one.

¡Dios mío! she thought, nearly screaming it.

P.O.W.G. #2's blood-caked corpse was slumped over a lidless toilet. Even after years at this grisly job, Hermosa could still feel horror.

"Fitzgerald?" she said, shivering, into her radio. "I need backup."

At that moment, Hermosa's phone vibrated and blared with a contact-specific ringtone. Her wife. Bad timing, but she answered. In case this was goodbye.

"Can't talk for long, love," Hermosa said, all but whispering. "This negotiation has...stalled."

"That's why I called, Ariana," her wife said. "I'm watching the news—do those kids really have suicide belts on?!"

"A vest...just one of them...we think." Perhaps this was not the right time for honesty, Hermosa decided.

"You're not going *in* there, are you?"

"I..." Hermosa paused. "No, I'm perfectly safe. So far back from the action, it could be a desk job."

"Good, because our baby *won't* lose a mommy before he's born. Promise me, Ariana."

"We'll be a happy family very soon." Hermosa winced. She had to change the subject. "Olivia Oldman didn't remember me, isn't that funny? If only she knew that you and I met by talking shit about her after class..."

As Hermosa's wife laughed, the agent realized with a jolt that she wasn't alone in the restroom.

"I can let Professor Olivia know for you," Caleb said, blocking the door. His finger hovered above the detonator of his vest. "Oh, I'll be taking your phone now. And your walkie-talkie. I'm not afraid to push this button."

Hermosa lowered the communication devices and slid them to Caleb with her foot. Too blindsided for hypnotic induction, she resorted to cliché. "You...have so much to live for, kid."

"Don't. Call. Me. *Kid*." He slammed a fist against the paper towel dispenser, breaking it open. "Got a gun?"

"No...I don't take firearms into negotiations."

"*Liar*." Caleb grazed his thumb across the detonator. "Do you *all* think 'young' means 'gullible'?"

Hermosa knew that Caleb was ready for death, ready to share it with others. This was no stunt for attention, no cry for help. Not like Alex at the high school earlier. "Wait..." She lifted her pant leg to reveal Alex's Glock; there hadn't been time to bag it for evidence.

"What I thought," Caleb said. "I'll be taking that, too."

50.

"*Why* do you need backup?" Fitzgerald yelled into his radio. "Hermosa...? Are you still there?"

No response. He had sworn to never lose another soldier in the line of duty, and though he would not admit it to Hermosa—out of refusal to feed millennial addiction to praise—she was his best.

"This campus is no longer a safe space." Fitzgerald grabbed the nearby SWAT captain. "We're going in. Let's give those freshmen scum a *real* orientation; let's bring their generation to heel."

"I'm Gen X, man," the SWAT captain said. "This whole millennial versus boomer war is just exhausting if you're halfway between. It's like nobody even remembers *us* anymore."

"Load the grenades, you slacker!"

51.

Ash, Jackson, Nikki, Meg, and Pablo waited in the history classroom for Olivia to return.

"Your face looks busted, bro," Ash said to Jackson. They had both taken rough hits in their scuffle.

"Not as busted as yours'll look," Jackson said, "if you mention my face one more time."

"Guys, Professor Olivia said no fighting," Pablo interrupted them. "Well, technically she said, 'No fighting, meatheads.'"

"When do you think she'll come back?" Meg said, checking her engagement metrics and new follower count, and then compulsively checking them again to calm her nerves.

"Major economic reform might take longer than you'd expect," Nikki said.

"Oh," Meg said, "it's like when you upload a video to YouTube and you think it's ready to watch, but then it says 'processing' for another hour."

"Yeah...just like that." Nikki's face held both contempt and concern. "Look, I spend too much time online instead of IRL myself—Tumblr, mostly—but do you ever think you might have a problem?"

"Um, hello?" Meg said. "The internet *is* IRL now...it's *better* than IRL. I have a following, okay? And that means I'm relevant. My voice *matters*. And if your voice *doesn't* matter—if you *aren't* relevant—then it's like you never existed at all, so *leave me alone*."

Her classmates sat in uncomfortable silence. She checked the metrics again.

Caleb marched Hermosa into the classroom, gun

pointed at her back. "The FBI knows about the dead professor," he said as the other students jumped in their seats.

"*Shit*," Jackson said.

"None of us had anything to do with that, okay?" Nikki told Hermosa. "Except for Jackson, who had everything to do with that."

"What the hell, Nikki?" Jackson said. "Fuck you, I'm going to jail now."

"Damn straight..." Hermosa turned towards Caleb. "And so are you."

Caleb gagged Hermosa with a whiteboard eraser. "We're on the right side of history," he said, tying the agent to a chair with leftover twine. "That means nothing we do is a crime, only an acceleration of progress."

He eyed the guillotine. Yes, it was time.

"Watch her," Caleb told Jackson. "BRB."

52.

Olivia entered the staff lounge, feeling triumphant. "Good news!" she said. "I cut a deal with Senator Ellis...y'know, *the* Senator Ellis? Homegirl just has to fly back to D.C., count the votes, and then we'll let you go."

"Is that so?" Dean Oldman said, voice full of skepticism. "Our missing colleague is taking quite the bathroom break, Olivia."

A guilty chill shot through Olivia's body. "Yeah, uh, he loves his fiber bars...gotta stay regular...but this crisis is almost over."

"This crisis never should've happened in the first place," Dean Oldman said. "You of all people should know a saying from late 1700s France: 'The Revolution devours its children.'"

"I'm proud of you, dear," Linda said, "for choosing the diplomatic path. Your idealism makes *me* feel young again, as much as I'd rather be at home right now. You've handled this difficult day very well."

"Thanks, Linda...actually, you know what?" Olivia cut the twine from her favorite colleague's hands and feet. "*Go* home."

"What about the rest of us?" said P.O.W.G. #3. "Can *I* go?"

"'About time these spoiled millennials heard the word *no*,' remember that one?" Olivia said. "Well, now *you* get to hear it."

Linda walked towards the door and then paused. "Your students have such wonderful, radical passion, Olivia," she said, "but our job as educators is to help them move beyond mere fervor. To help them find themselves. So first, we must find *our*selves. Remember that."

Linda closed the door behind her so softly that it didn't make a sound.

"He's dead, isn't he?" Dean Oldman asked Olivia, nodding towards P.O.W.G. #2's empty seat at the table. "Not still, hours later, in the bathroom? Is *that* how one of those brutes 'messed up—like, real bad'? I can see it on your face."

Olivia bit her lip. Tears of remorse welled in her eyes. "It was an accident, Daddy."

She was no longer a revolutionary. Nor even an adult. Just a little girl, scared and ashamed.

"You aren't my daughter," Dean Oldman said. "Not anymore. All you are is a series of compounding disappointments. I'm almost *relieved* that your mother couldn't see how you turned out."

Olivia ran away, teardrops bursting.

53.

With a screwdriver in the Department of Art and Design supply closet, Caleb detached the paper cutter's blade. "Time for some staffing cuts," he said to himself.

This would make good ol' Mr. Kaczynski proud. No batteries, no computer processors, just the razor's edge.

On his way to the staff lounge to retrieve the oppressors, Caleb saw Linda in the hallway. "Who said *you* could go free...?"

54.

The SWAT captain loaded a smoke grenade—the first of many—into the launcher.

"You sure about this?" he said to Fitzgerald. "They're...y'know...kids. How dangerous can they be?"

"I wasn't a 'kid' when Uncle Sam sent me to 'Nam," Fitzgerald said. "I was a *man*, old enough to kill and *be* killed. Just like they are now."

Fitzgerald grimaced. Nobody here knew the *truth* except for him. They were all too weak, sheltered, and coddled to *begin* to understand it. There was nothing innocent about youth. What he had seen at that age, what he had *done*...he could still hear the screams. And, truth be told, he still enjoyed them.

"Fire!" Fitzgerald ordered.

55.

Such a fuck-up, Olivia cursed herself. She was curled in a corner of the lobby. *I'm just a stupid, shortsighted asshole who made every wrong choice a person could ever make, ruined her own life, got another life snuffed out, and now—*

All electricity went off inside the Main Hall except for the emergency lights. Smoke grenades careened at a shrieking decibel level through every window. The crime scene had become a war zone. Olivia curled even tighter out of survival instinct.

"Come out *now*, punks," Fitzgerald's voice boomed through a loudspeaker. "Failure to comply in the next thirty seconds will result in deadly force."

Olivia forced herself to unroll. She felt her way back upstairs through the dark haze, coughing hard, dragging her feet to avoid stepping on the mystery boxes. She had to get back to her students, to protect them. In the hallway she gripped the history classroom doorknob. Turned it. Walked inside.

A nightmare scene awaited her: Linda was trapped in the guillotine's lunette headlock; Caleb had attached the paper cutter's blade to the weight above. Ash, Nikki, Meg, and Pablo—but not Jackson—were tied on the floor, now hostages themselves beside

Dean Oldman, P.O.W.G. #3, and Hermosa. The air was thick with a unique kind of fear. An enfeebling fear. The fear of impending massacre.

"Professor..." Caleb grinned. "You're just in time."

CHAPTER ELEVEN

56.

Benjy watched from behind the police line. *Is all of this chaos my fault?* he wondered. If he had stayed inside with Olivia instead of running away at the first sign of trouble, could he have kept the situation under control with a less belligerent PR strategy?

Stop being a coward, he told himself. *Stop being a coward, stop being a...*

As a child, Benjy had run from bullies at Hebrew school, who mocked him for being half-Asian, and from his cousins in Osaka, who mocked him for being half-*gaijin*. As an adult, he had run from insisting on his own basic labor rights. No more running from problems; it was time to run towards one, to help Olivia and the students. *Stop. Being. A. Coward.*

Benjy summoned his courage and sprinted for the Main Hall.

"Stop what you're doing," the SWAT captain called out.

"I just did!" Benjy said, entering the building. Normally the liveliest spot on campus, it felt sinister now, a place of dread, of doom. "WWJMD? What would John McClane do?"

He groped around the smoky darkness of the lobby for the elevator; its first-floor doors were open, an automatic security precaution triggered when the lights went out.

"Nakatomi Plaza, going up..." Benjy attempted to open the emergency hatch and climb up the shaft—like Bruce Willis did in the 1988 Christmas action classic licensed on his underwear—but immediately fell seven feet back down. "Fuck!" Benjy said midair.

The impact knocked him unconscious.

57.

Caleb slid his finger up and down the grooves of the guillotine that held Linda in place. "My classmates opposed this final solution to the baby boomer question," he told Olivia. "Jackson understood though, didn't you?"

"It is what it is, bro," Jackson said with an expression of stone.

"Yo," Ash said, "why are you acting like this dick's henchman?"

"All I know is Caleb's the *only* one who has my back," Jackson said. "The only one who didn't want to turn me in."

"It's all about you, huh? That's what it comes down to, bro?"

Jackson looked away, ashamed but unable to face it.

Hermosa tried to speak through her gag; it was futile.

"Can't negotiate your way out of this one," Caleb said.

"Caleb," Olivia said, "we *had* a way out of this. We still do."

"That deal was a Band-Aid on a severed jugular —speaking of which..." Caleb propped Meg's smartphone horizontally on a desk and began streaming. "Welcome to the show, my acolytes. Welcome to the revolution." He knelt face-to-face with Linda. "Boomers love their stocks, so I'm putting them *in* stocks."

"Olivia, I—" Linda began to say.

"And you know the first rule of investing?" Caleb broke her off. "Never catch a falling knife."

He stood and released the blade, decapitating Linda with a swift, almost clean slice. Everybody screamed as her head—eyelids and lips still twitching—dangled from a sinew, split, and rolled into a trashcan. Jackson had killed earlier in self-defense, but Caleb's act now was calculated, coldblooded murder.

"*Linda*!" Olivia's legs wobbled with terror and nausea; her eyes gushed with salty sobs. "Oh my God, oh Christ, no no no no *no*...what the *fuck*, you little psycho?"

"Professor Olivia, I know this isn't a good time," Nikki said through her own tears, "but I'm calling you out! 'Psycho' is ableist, stigmatizing language...it's super problematic."

"Okay, Nikki, you know what else is 'problematic'?" Olivia said. "*Talking*. Talking is problematic, and while we need to confront actual bigotry, if you critique every little thing that anybody says—even if they're on your side, even if their heart is in the right place—you're just going to push them away. And personally, I'm so sick and tired of pushing people away, because it ends with...*this*."

Nikki was stunned. "Did...did you just call me out?"

Jackson tried to start a slow clap, having apparently forgotten that the bound others could not join in.

Footsteps in the hallway. Police boots. Caleb withdrew a remote control from his pocket.

The box, Olivia thought, bracing herself. *All of those tiny boxes.*

58.

Fitzgerald and the SWAT officers rushed towards the classroom, ready to storm in. They hadn't anticipated Caleb's handcrafted blitzkrieg.

KAAAAA-*BOOOOOOOOOOOM*.

Limbs and viscera splattered everywhere. Fitzgerald looked around. He was the team's only survivor.

59.

Students and professors flinched with each successive explosion of the onslaught. The sound of high-velocity nails—*veeeeeeeeeew, veeeeeeeeeew*—mingled with sounds of high-pitched necrotic suffering. A stench of gunpowder and charred barbecue filled the air. A stench of war. A stench of hell.

"What in the shit was *that*?" Nikki said after the cacophony had ended.

"A little surprise for the FBI," Caleb said. "Good ol' Mr. Kaczynski didn't see 'em coming, but I did."

"You do realize your hero, the Unabomber, *is* a baby boomer?" Olivia said.

"The only one worth sparing..." Caleb removed Linda's headless body from the guillotine and shoved P.O.W.G. #3 into it.

"Please, I can pay off your debt myself," begged the professor. "What is it, a hundred thousand? A hundred and fifty? That's my Roth IRA...my retirement fund. Take it. Take all of it. There's a tax penalty for early withdrawal, but—"

"I'm only taking one thing from you." Caleb pulled the déclic release mechanism, but the blade—already warped from Linda's vertebrae—fell only halfway through the professor's neck; it was meant for cutting through paper, not bone and tendons. Caleb nevertheless pressed the blade down the rest of the way like a saw; blood squirted in all directions, drenching him in a warm crimson shower, a coppery viscous geyser. "I guess you could call him an *absent-minded* professor, LOL."

The witnesses, young and old, cried out again. More screams, more snot-drenched blubbering.

"Caleb, this isn't a 'revolution,'" Olivia said. "It's a *slaughter*. You have to stop."

"*They* won't stop destroying our world," Caleb said. "They're like beasts who—beasts *that*—eat their young, beasts that *require* slaughter. If we want to live to our ripe old age, then *theirs* must end. Youth power! Youth power!"

Dean Oldman was next on the chopping block.

"Caleb, it's my dad," Olivia said. "I don't always like him, but I still love him. Please. You can't."

"No, *you* can't, because you're *weak*," Caleb said. "But I'll help you to become strong."

"Honey..." Dean Oldman fought back his own weeping; Olivia had only seen him cry once before, at her mother's funeral. "I sold out for you."

"What...?" Olivia said.

"You asked the other night why I did it—cut my long hair, stopped fighting the system and joined in," Dean Oldman said. "It's because your mom and I had you. We wanted to always be there, to give you a good life, even if it meant exchanging my tie-dye for a necktie, and mowing grass instead of smoking it. We became mundane grown-ups for *you*. And I know we let you down, and I'm sorry...I'm sorry for blaming your generation when it's mine who failed. I'm sorry for this dying world. I'm sorry we weren't able to give you the one that we dreamed of. Because you deserved it. You were *entitled* to it."

"Daddy..." Olivia could not find the words.

"*Enough*, oppressor," Caleb said, reaching for the déclic. "You're toast."

Toast... It tugged at Olivia's memory. *The avocado on the desk.* She grabbed it. Hurled it with the muscle memory of her varsity aim.

Daddy...

The blade fell.

I love you...

The avocado spun through the air.

I forgive you.

The omega-3-rich produce landed on the back of Dean Oldman's neck. A fraction of a second later, the warped blade—with a blunt thump—caught in the middle of a round, thick, brown pit. The roomful of hostages let out a collective sigh.

"Hell of a throw," Dean Oldman said, larynx squeezed from the pressure. It clearly was the worst physical pain that he'd ever felt—since the nightstick, anyway—but he would live.

"You taught me how, Coach," Olivia said. "By the way, that speech was woke AF."

"What does 'AF' mean?" asked the dean.

"As father." They shared an all-too-brief smile.

"*Traitor...*" Caleb, seething with cosmic rage, pointed the Glock at Olivia. "I *knew* you were one of them—just another self-centered dinosaur—but I'm your fucking asteroid."

"Professor Olivia isn't 'self-centered,'" Pablo said, forcing himself upright despite his bindings. "She's done everything for us, risked everything she has."

"She's risked nothing, *sacrificed* nothing," Caleb said. "But it's time she did."

He squeezed the trigger.

"*Professor Olivia, no...*" Pablo jumped in front of the bullet. It pierced through his stomach and ricocheted off the lunette lock. He crashed to the ground, leaking a puddle of biofluids.

Olivia's heart ached. "Oh God, Pablo, why?"

"I...just..." He gurgled. "Wanted...to...help."

His eyes rolled back. Gone. *More innocent blood on our hands*, she thought. *The most innocent. On my hands for convincing anyone to believe in me.*

"How *could* you?" Nikki shouted at Caleb.

"Pablo was *one* of us," Meg said.

"I *loved* that little bro," Ash said.

"I...I didn't mean to..." Caleb stammered, but then shook the doubt out of his head. "Pablo was a traitor, too. He tried to protect our *oppressors*."

"I'm calling you out!" Nikki said. "*You're* oppressing *us* right now."

"All you do is judge others," Caleb said, "but you won't judge the *guilty*?"

Olivia walked forward until the still-hot Glock barrel pressed against her sternum. "You want to kill me because I'm older than you, Caleb?" she said. "Then kill me. Maybe I even deserve it for being so selfish all of these years—I *was* self-centered, I can admit that now—but do *not* hurt one more of my students."

Dean Oldman watched his daughter, open-jawed with a mix of fear and pride. Even if he were to die today, he had lived to see her shine. Frantic to save his only child, his only family left, he struggled against the weight of the wood; it shifted above his neck. The ricocheted bullet had loosened the guillotine's stocks. He could wriggle out.

"Like *you* care, Professor," Caleb said, trigger finger quivering. "The dean's own daughter, privileged from birth—just another master on the plantation—growing dumber and crueler with each passing, withering day."

"I dunno, Caleb, this all sounds a little immature," Olivia said. "Maybe you'll get some perspective in a few years?"

Caleb's finger steadied. He took a step back and took aim. "You won't be around to know, Professor…"

The gun fired. Its bullet struck the ceiling as Dean Oldman grabbed Caleb and chucked him out of the classroom window. The suicide vest detonated against the granite steps below with a near-blinding flash and a near-deafening burst of flame and metal.

"You're expelled, kid," the dean said.

Olivia covered her eyes and ears, running into her father's arms. "None of it was supposed to happen this way…" She shook with trauma. "I…I don't know what I was th…th…"

"Whatever you were thinking," Dean Oldman said, "you got it from me."

"Hey, no rush—totally Instagrammable moment and all," Meg said with a nervous laugh. "But could you two, like, free us?"

A notification on her phone's screen read: *Account Terminated for Violent Content*. Upon seeing it, she screamed louder than anybody else that day.

60.

Jackson fled into the hallway at top athletic speed. With Caleb gone, nobody—not even his own brother—would protect him anymore.

"*FBI*!" Fitzgerald said, gun drawn. "Get on the ground."

Jackson ignored the order and lunged towards Fitzgerald. He had already killed one geezer today with his bare hands; he could do it again.

"You know the difference between college and the real world, son?" Fitzgerald said, aiming his pistol at Jackson's torso. "No trigger warnings."

BLAM. BLAM. BLAM. BLAM. With the hint of a smile on his lips, Fitzgerald filled numerous vital organs with lead. Hunter and prey.

"Bro...?" said Ash, peeking into the hallway. "*Bro*!" He ran to cradle Jackson's ammunition-pockmarked body. With the vanquished SWAT team scattered around them, it was impossible to tell where one victim's pool of blood ended and the next victim's began, a mass grave in need of dirt.

"I'm s...sor...sorry..." Jackson's voice was a foamy, saliva-sodden whimper. "You're m...my boy..."

Ash wept. "You're *my* boy. We're good. We're good, bro." But his brother was no longer alive to hear it.

Fitzgerald walked past and saw the decapitated bodies on the classroom floor. "My God..." He pointed his gun at Ash, Nikki, and then Meg. "I knew you hooligans were out of your minds."

"Do it," Meg said. "I already died tonight with my social."

"*Whoa*, man," Nikki said. "The killer was Caleb, not us."

"You're *all* killers—you *love* it," Fitzgerald said. "Some jury full of suckers will take pity on your naïve, easily misled age, but *I* know the truth."

"They didn't do anything wrong," Olivia said.

"This pile of bodies on the floor implies otherwise," Fitzgerald said. "Millennials really *do* hate reality, don't you? Well, I'm happy to give you a dose of it. We had *our* Kent State, now it's time for yours."

A now-conscious Benjy pried the elevator doors open and tackled Fitzgerald from behind, knocking the pistol across the floor. "Yippee ki-*yay*, motherf—"

Fitzgerald elbowed Benjy in the solar plexus, but it gave Ash an opening to put the lawman in a chokehold.

"He...was...my...*brother*." Ash squeezed hard. "*You. Killed. My. Brother.*"

"Hermosa!" Fitzgerald gasped for air. "Stop them. Free me. End this now."

"This—*is*—ended," Hermosa said, her voice slowing to the tempo and rising to the pitch of a lullaby. "*We* are free. You stop. *Now*."

"'We'? '*We*'?" Fitzgerald's skin turned purple. "Did

you g...go full...Stockholm Syndrome? Sym...pathizing with...your *captors*?"

"My only captor was a mountain of student debt," Hermosa said. "But we—don't—have—to—be—held—captive—anymore, do we?"

"E...vil..." Fitzgerald's skin turned purple. "Your...gener...a...tion..."

"I helped *fight* an evil here today," Hermosa said. "A crime *against* my generation."

Fitzgerald was losing consciousness. "You'll...nev...er work...for the Bureau...again."

"Neither will you. Happy retirement."

Fitzgerald tapped out. Ash let him go. Still alive. No eye for an eye. No more death.

"Thanks for the assist, Benjy," Olivia said. "But why didn't you just take the stairs?"

"I...I..." He wheezed, clutching his abdomen. "WWJMD?"

"Hold up," Olivia said, lifting her phone. She had received a bank notification: *TRAVIS Z. has sent you $2,000,000.* The device then buzzed with a call. Travis's profile pic. She answered.

"Hey babe, did that transfer go through?" Travis said. "For the Alzheimer's fundraiser or something?"

"Yeah...uh...debt relief," Olivia said. "But I told you we didn't need it?"

"Look, babe, every penny helps, right? So just keep it for whatever stuff you need, no worries. I make a couple mil before breakfast every morning; I've probably made a couple mil during this phone call. When I say I'm balls deep in cash, babe, I mean *balls* deep. Like, if cash were my penis and I were having sex with a vagina, my testicles would literally be deep inside of it...the vagina, I mean, not the cash. Why would my testicles be deep inside of cash? That doesn't even make *sense*."

"Oh..." Olivia blinked. "Right."

"Gotta split, babe, Marky Mark Zucker-B. is on line two. *Ciao!*"

Travis disconnected. Olivia stood speechless.

61.

Enormous crowds of joyous youth celebrated in the streets nationwide, singing, dancing, and burning their copies of federal loan promissory notes. The images, televised live on cable news, were as instantly iconic as those from V-J Day and the fall of the Berlin Wall.

"It was the largest demonstration of civil disobedience on U.S. college campuses in fifty years—and the most effective," the young anchor said.

"Today, Congress approved the National Student Debt Relief Act, providing a *new* New Deal to millions of Americans. Senate Banking Committee Chairwoman Brenda Jane Ellis, who cast the deciding vote, called it 'just the right thing to do for our kids,' a sharp reversal that all but guarantees her reelection based on the latest polling. On a personal note, I'd like to offer the senator an apology for my unprofessional, albeit massively viral, remarks from earlier this week."

"Financial stocks were surprisingly *up* on the news," the old anchor said. "Few saw it coming, but this might boost the economy thanks to a windfall for millennial entrepreneurship and home ownership. And perhaps the market is satisfied that this divisive, uncertain chapter is over."

The footage cut to body bags in Olivia's history classroom.

"However, it comes at a steep price," the young anchor said. "Three students and three professors died in clashes at Logan Frost University. None of the surviving undergrads partook in the violence, according to the Justice Department, which suspended the local FBI field office director for allegations of excessive force during the rescue operation. Logan Frost's trustees have declined to press charges against Professor Olivia Oldman for her role, with its dean—her father, Mitchell Oldman—calling for a time of unity and healing."

The old anchor extended a hand. "I'll do my part."

They shook on it.

ONE YEAR LATER

62.

The controversial statue of a World War I chemical weapons engineer no longer stood on the quad. A statue of Pablo had taken its place. Olivia spoke at a podium for the unveiling.

"Teachers like to say that we learn more from our students than they do from us," she told the audience of hundreds. "That's...not always super true."

Muted laughter from the crowd.

"But Pablo taught me about gentleness," Olivia said. "He was so gentle and so shy. When the time came, he stood up for what's right...with his words and his deeds, but never with violence."

She paused, dreading the next paragraph of her remarks.

"Two more of my students died that day. I refuse to say one's name…but the other, Jackson, was truly in the wrong place at the wrong time. I also want to honor my colleagues—including my dear friend Linda—who lost their lives over a terrible misunderstanding. We all need to listen better. I'll practice what I preach: less acting like I know everything, more asking what I don't.

"Evil doesn't have an age. It can live inside of us no matter how old or how young we are. Human nature won't change, which is why we have to learn from our elders; they've seen more of it. In return, our elders have to leave us with a better world, a *sustainable* world of hope, of opportunity. We've all failed one another, but it's not too late to try again. I know that's what Pablo would want…and it's what I want."

She left the podium to the sound of a standing ovation.

63.

Benjy walked up to Olivia after the speech. They had not spoken in twelve months. Too many bad memories. "Hi…"

"Hey comrade," she said.

"Nice tribute up there."

"Thanks...I just wish I'd never had a reason to write it."

"So, are you doing okay?"

"I've been seeing a therapist," Olivia said. "The nightmares are a little less frequent. And I'm figuring out a lot, too, about myself...about learned helplessness. Not easy for a teacher, but I'm trying to *un*learn it."

"Olivia, I'm sorry I ran out of there when things started getting bad," Benjy said. "I was a coward, I—"

"You were *right*, Benjy. Nobody thinks they're a 'monster' until they look in a mirror and see one staring back. That's my burden now, not yours."

"You're not a monster, Olivia."

"Hey, I'm a monster in the sack, aren't I?" She winked. "At least, on the table?"

Benjy laughed. "You really don't blame me for leaving?"

"I'm trying to blame people less in general," Olivia said. "Nobody's perfect. I mean, I'm the biggest fuck-up on this campus, right?"

"'Fuck up'...?" Benjy said. "You liberated *millions* of us. You're, like, our Moses—except without a beard."

"My Prince Charming over here."

"Our first date wasn't a success."

"Maybe our second one will be?"

"Second...?" Benjy blushed. "Is that *a* date or dat*ing*?"

Ash, Meg, and Nikki interrupted their flirtation.

"Thanks for giving my bro a shout out, Professor," Ash said. "He wasn't a bad dude, just cracked under pressure, you know?"

"I know, Ash," Olivia said. "Any of us could have."

"It's just...he was half of me. And now I need to figure out who I am without him."

"Losing family is the hardest thing in the world, so we've gotta stay tight with the ones who are still here..." Olivia paused. "'Tight,' did I say it correctly? Was that proper usage of the word 'tight'?"

"Yeah," Ash said, "that was tight."

Meg flipped a vintage Razr phone open and shut, open and shut.

"What is *that*?" Olivia asked her. "It still *works*? Those don't even have the internet...you aren't documenting every moment of your existence?"

"Oh, I threw my smartphone in the trash," Meg said. "Once I got rid of that garbage, I realized how addicted and miserable it was making me. Likes, comments, shares...who cares?" She flipped the phone open again. "Plus, this thing is *super* fun to play around with."

"Amazing," Olivia said.

"It's retro!" Meg chirped.

"You hear that, Olivia?" Benjy said. "*Our* youth is 'retro' now."

"Oh no, I can't," Olivia said. "Hashtag #ICannot."

"Yo, Professor Olivia," Nikki said, "I'm calling y—"

"Ugh, Nikki, what are you calling me out for now?"

"No, I mean, I'll *call* you sometime. I'm trying to work on my conversation skills—like, talking *with* people, not just *at* them?"

"Talking? On the phone? With your voice?" Olivia shook her head. "That *is* retro."

64.

Olivia strolled into the Main Hall, ready to meet her new batch of pupils, but first ducked into the classroom next to hers. A psychology course was in progress.

"And just like in a hostage crisis," Hermosa

lectured to dozens of students, "that's how you negotiate *any* aspect of life, from salaries to roommates to relationships. Never bargain from weakness, because what earns you respect is inner strength."

The former FBI agent took a sip of coffee from a mug inscribed "WORLD'S SECOND BEST MOM."

"All right, class, next week's reading is Chapter Two," Hermosa said. "Don't forget, your essays are due Wednesday."

The students walked towards the exit, including Alex—now a college freshman—holding hands with a girlfriend.

"Alex, what a wonderful surprise," Hermosa said to him.

"Hi Ariana," Alex said. "Or should I call you Professor?"

"Hmm..." She smiled at Olivia. "Professor Ariana has a nice ring."

"Thanks for testifying about that Fitzgerald prick," Alex said. "You really got the jury on my side."

"My pleasure," Hermosa said. "So, you're not an 'incel' anymore? No more teen angst?"

"Naaah...you were right about college. It's way more chill here. I learned how to *be* more chill here—it's kind of a funny story, I guess." Alex's girlfriend tugged on his arm. "I have to get to my next class, Professor Ariana, but...yeah, just, like, thanks again for everything. You're a lifesaver."

"Damn, girl," Olivia said to Hermosa after Alex had left, "you are a *natural*."

"I still miss the Bureau sometimes," Hermosa said, "but you know what? I *like* this teaching gig you lined up. Not all of the kids get what I'm trying to convey, but the ones who do, they make it worth it."

"Exactly!" Olivia said. "You'll only reach so many students, but whenever that happens..."

"The world changes."

Olivia nodded. "Plus, we've got tenure-track now, so...can't be fired for annnnnnything soon."

"If *you* still have a job here," Hermosa said, "I'm really not worried about my own."

65.

Dean Oldman packed a career's worth of belongings in his office.

"Wow, I can't believe it," Olivia said. "The old goat—I mean, the G.O.A.T.—is actually retiring. End of an era!"

"'G.O.A.T.'?" Dean Oldman asked.

"Greatest of all time. It's *peak* dope."

"Ah...I've wanted to call it a day for years," Dean Oldman said. "Time to give the next generation a chance to run things. Besides, now I can go out on a high note."

He showed Olivia a year-old, framed newspaper with the headline, "Hero College Dean Saves Students from Unabomber Copycat."

"When does the dean *ever* get to be a hero?" he said. "We're the villain in every damn college movie!"

"You're not a villain, Dad," Olivia said. "C'mon, I'll walk you outside."

She helped Dean Oldman carry his memorabilia from the Main Hall.

"I've gotta deal with my own move after this," Olivia said. She had bought a modest one-story home with a tenth of Travis's gift and donated the rest, in Pablo's name, to a legal assistance nonprofit for DREAMers.

"It'll be a lot quieter around the house without you," Dean Oldman said. "But swing by for dinner anytime."

"You mean swing by and *cook* dinner?" Olivia said.

"Oh, I'll cook...it's not the 1950s anymore." The dean paused. "I'm proud of you, Olivia. Mom would be, too. You've grown up so much."

"Thanks, Pops. Hashtag #Adulting."

"Maybe cut it out with the hashtags, though?"

On the steps, Dean Oldman raised his fists for old times' sake. "Youth power!" the seventy-year-old bellowed.

"Dad, you're such a dork..." Olivia laughed. "I love it."

66.

Olivia parked her Prius in the carport and set a stack of boxes on the suburban porch. The house would need kitchen renovations, bathroom renovations, and who knew what else, but it was hers...*her* house. Finally.

Turning a key in the lock—it took a few attempts to learn the correct jiggling pattern—she prepared tomorrow's lecture in her mind:

In college, I didn't understand why my professors were still obsessed with Vietnam, Watergate, Woodstock, and all the rest decades later. Same story with my father. What did it have to do with the modern world? Why couldn't they move on from ancient history? Now I get it. That was their struggle, their moment, their revolution...just as we've had ours. New generations will learn about this era in future textbooks, but only we'll be able to truly understand it, to fully grasp it—what we've gained, what we've lost, and how we've found our way home.

She walked inside and closed the door.

ABOUT THE AUTHOR

Marty Beckerman is a #1 Amazon.com bestselling humorist. *USA Today* calls his writing "laugh-out-loud" and *Business Insider* calls him "the most famous author" from Alaska. A former editor at *Esquire* and MTV News, Beckerman has also written for the *New York Times*, the *Atlantic*, *Wired*, *Playboy*, *Discover*, *Maxim*, CBS Interactive, *Mental Floss*, the *Daily Beast*, and other leading publications. He lives in Los Angeles with his wife and their cat and Netflix.

Made in the USA
Lexington, KY
11 February 2019